The Fourth Estate Murders

To Marilyn
from Lauren

The Fourth Estate Murders

by
Ed Calandro

Pierpont Publishing / Connecticut

PUBLISHED BY
Pierpont Publishing, Inc.
500 Howe Avenue
Shelton, Connecticut 06484

THE FOURTH ESTATE MURDERS

Manufactured in the the United States of America.

First Printing: February 1993
1 2 3 4 5 6 7 8 9 10

LIBRARY OF CONGRESS CATALOGING-IN-PUBLICATION DATA:
Library of Congress Catalog Card Number: 93-85173
Calandro, Ed, 1944.
    The Fourth Estate murders / Ed Calandro.
    p.   cm.
    ISBN 1-884520-00-6
    I. Title.
    813'.54—dc20

Typography by Carolyn Calandro

**For my brother Chub,
the core of our family tree.**

AUTHOR'S NOTE

Ordinarily there is no need for a preface for a novel . . . I was born in Bridgeport, Connecticut which is in the heart of Fairfield County. Back in the Fifties it was the richest county, per capita, in the United States. Not Bridgeport itself though. Bridgeport was just factory after factory. All of us who lived there were, in one way or another, connected to a factory. We were the blue collar-blue apron people.

We used every ethnic slur imaginable to describe each other. It's funny, but when I left Bridgeport I found it baffling how other communities viewed the way inner city people spoke to one another. You know—the better educated, affluent communities.

In Bridgeport there was no need for bussing because we all went to the same schools. There was no need for welfare because we all worked. There were no need for psychologists or analysts because we were mostly happy and too busy.

We made everything: the weapons, the farm equipment, the appliances, flying- and ground-assault machines; we even made a good share of the smog.

It was a matriarchal society. The men worked, so did the woman. But the woman also raised us, fed us and guided us.

Now Bridgeport is a city of vacant factories—hugh, hollow, brick structures. The blue collar-blue apron people who once paid the mighty tax dollar for a good part of the state are gone. But the language spoken there, and in many other forgotten industrial cities, remains the same. . . .

ONE

I was in a frenzy to get my office in order. In less than a hour Mr. Remsen Barnes was expected here. I presumed he was interested in my services. Since he owned a major girdle and bra factory here in Bridgeport, hopefully he'd hire me to investigate pilfering within his organization. Anything as long as it wasn't another divorce case. I'd spent the last twelve years following adulterous spouses and investigating fraudulent insurance swindles. A wealthy client, that's what I wanted, and Mr. Barnes certainly qualified in that category.

My office was also my home. Rarely did I invite clients up here. Usually I'd meet them in a bar, at their homes, or in offices. But Remsen Barnes' secretary had insisted that he meet me here.

I had the radio on loud, listening to the news. Bush and his allies had been bombing the city of Baghdad all night. We were still at war. The radio news had grabbed my interest to the point where I didn't even realize someone had entered the room. That was until the sweet scent of a perfume caused my eyes to flutter. Then came her voice, "'Scusi, Signore Conte."

With a dirty sock dangling from my hand, I turned to see a quite-attractive, young lady standing at the doorway. "Oh, yes— um, hello—please come in." I couldn't help but notice what a voluptuous body she had as she moved shyly toward me.

"I hav-a di big problema wid di Inglese. Parla Italiano?"

"Jeez, I'm sorry, I don't. A few words, no more."

THE FOURTH ESTATE MURDERS

Her expression saddened, "Oh mio, that-a non buono."

She was gorgeous. What a body! I raised my finger to indicate she should wait. "Stay right here, please, I have an Italian-English dictionary in the next room." She gave me an understanding smile. I shut off the news of the stupid war and hurried to find my dictionary. When I returned with the book, she had seated herself on my couch. I saw no reason to sit behind my desk instead of sitting next to her. This bold maneuver seemed to please her, but not as much as it did me.

I requested that she speak slowly and use all the English she knew in her talk. For a moment she didn't say anything, staring deep into my eyes. Then knowing she had my complete attention, she offered, "Mi name Gina Cataliano; mi husband, Bruno."

That's all she could say before the tears started rolling down her cheeks. I couldn't help myself; I dropped the dictionary and placed my arm around her hoping to comfort her, and at the same time feeling blessed to be close enough for my nostrils to devour her delicious scent. But to my despair her face seemed to grimace with disapproval. I quickly removed my arm thinking I had certainly moved too fast.

Gina noticed my discomfort and was quick to put me at ease.

"No, no, Signore Conte, it not-a you."

"Please, Gina, don't think the wrong thing; and my name is James, but everyone calls me Jimmy."

She nodded her understanding. "Si, Jemme, how mi tell-a you? I hav-a di hurt on mi tettas e mi fica." She placed her hands gently over her bosom which helped me to figure out what the tettas were. I grabbed the dictionary and quickly turned the pages looking for the word "fica". When I found it, I almost choked on my saliva. It was a slang word for vagina. I looked at Gina Cataliano in a different light. Once again she was quick to put my unease to rest. She took my hand and put it in hers between us on the couch. I hadn't realized how much makeup she had on until the tears wore a trail down her cheekbone.

For the next half hour she told me this gruesome tale of violence directed at her by her husband Bruno. With the aid of the dictionary and her slow speaking, I learned that on Saturdays her husband, Bruno, would leave early in the morning just like every other day; but for the past five Saturdays he'd been coming home very late—never saying anything. After he'd undress her, he'd grab her tettas and squeeze them until Gina screamed in pain. When he could not, in Gina's words—"bring-a di milk"—he would sit on the side on the bed and weep. But this last Saturday he had not cried, instead he had pinned his wife to the wall and kneed her many times in the fica.

I was horrified as Gina wept openly. Again I put my arm around her making sure to take care not to rub against the tettas or fica. She wanted help . . . but she only wanted to find out where Bruno went on Saturdays.

Was she ever good looking! She seemed to be comfortable resting her back on my arm and her head on my shoulder. I tried to explain to her how I worked. It would be a simple matter. I might be able to find out in one day where Bruno went on Saturdays. I had begun to discuss my fee just about the time I felt her foot moving slightly against my leg. For a moment I was startled and pulled away a little. I looked at Gina as she spoke, "Find-a where mi Bruno go. Please, Jemme."

"I'll try, Gina. But maybe you should go to the police."

She put her hands on my legs, half begging, "No, no! No polizia. I beg-a, Jemme. No polizia."

Before I could put her at ease, she had gotten down on her knees as if she felt she had to beg me not to call the police.

"It's okay, Gina. No police. Don't worry, there's no need to worry."

THE FOURTH ESTATE MURDERS

She put her face down on my knees. I thought she was going to begin weeping again. Instead she looked up at me, her eyes wet with sorrow. "I no hav-a monee, Jemme. I no hav."

I looked down at her as she ran her fingers between my legs up near "Hoppy" who was proudly erect, waiting to get in on this whole thing. She repeated herself, "I no hav-a monee." This time it seemed as if she was saying it directly to Hoppy, who responded spiritedly.

She rubbed it passionately, seemingly intent on freeing it from its clothed harness. With the lifting of the underwear, out it sprung in its glory. But in a moment it was hidden again, this time in Gina's mouth, sending me messages of wonderment as it continued to grow. As for Gina, she seemed to be enjoying it as much as "we" were, until I made the terrible mistake of reaching for one of her tettas—momentarily forgetting about Bruno's terrible misuse. She jumped, and as she did her teeth scraped against the skin, causing me more fear than harm. I must have had a ridiculous look on my face because as Gina got up off her knees, she began to giggle. Her dark eyes sparkled with amusement. Here she was, having used vulgar words such as fica and giving me head after knowing me for little more than half an hour, yet I felt embarrassed. Much to its dismay, I shoved Hoppy back inside my pants and closed the zipper. Gina's giggle turned into a sensuous smile. "No, Jemme, no put-a back, I like-a. But you hurt-a mi tettas."

I could say nothing before she was up against my body. Her scent was heavenly. "I like-a Jemme." She put her mouth onto mine, sticking her tongue deep inside. Hoppy started pushing hard to get out again. It ached and I knew if I didn't soon set it free it would explode inside. Gina stopped tickling my tonsils with her tongue for a moment to say, "I no hav-a monee, Jemme." She snickered in a suggestive way, then ran her tongue across my nose and down around the outer parts of my lips. She whispered, "Sodomita mi."

"Uh, what?"

"Sodomita mi, Jemme."

"I don't understand, Gina?"

Gina pulled away from me, never taking her eyes off my face. She began pulling up her skirt a little, then she reached behind her and seemed to be fiddling with her undergarments. She gave me one last sexy look, then turned around putting her hands on my desk while bending over. With one last pull she exposed her naked buttocks. "Pleese-a, Jemme, sodomita mi."

This was outrageous. I felt as if I had a wild cowboy between my legs anxious to mount up. I thought she could at least have bargained for my fee; all this really wasn't necessary. I felt helpless. I was afraid I was going to have to take her up on her generous offer. This was certainly a way of avoiding things, like not harming her tettas and fica. Or paying taxes on my fee.

If I hadn't already made my full share of blunders in my thirty-nine years, then I was in the process of making another one as Mr. Remsen Barnes walked through my unlocked door. There we were; thank God at least I was fully dressed. My only visible guilt was the bulge between my legs. Gina quickly stood up, frantically pulling her skirt down over the exposed derrière as the elderly, regal-looking Remsen Barnes stood in the doorway. It was hard to say if there was a genuine smile on his face or a corporate-type mask.

Gina spoke first. "Mi 'scusi, I go."

"Oh, um, let me get your number, Mrs. Cataliano."

"No, no, Signore Conte. Bruno no like-a that. I go." That was it. She picked up her purse and left.

The gray-haired, well-dressed gentleman closed the door after Gina's departure. "Mr. James Conte, I presume?"

THE FOURTH ESTATE MURDERS

I came walking to him with my hand extended. "Yes, and you must be Mr. Barnes." He nodded assent and with that I began to make excuses for what he had just witnessed. "I'm sorry about what you walked into, Mr. Barnes, but there's a good explanation."

"I assure you, Mr. Conte, you need not explain. I am not here to judge you on your personal habits. I am here to obtain your services. What you do with your other clients or in your private life is of no concern to me."

I was more than happy to sit down behind my desk, enabling me to conceal the bottom half of my body. Mr. Barnes took off his expensive-looking overcoat, revealing what was probably a thousand dollar suit underneath. He took a seat on the other side of the desk, lit up a cigarette and immediately began talking. "A little more than four months ago, my son, Morgan, was brutally murdered down by the Long Wharf in New Haven."

That's right, I had forgotten. His son was strangled on the wharf at New Haven Harbor. Remsen Barnes' lips trembled as he exhaled the smoke between them. "I'm afraid the New Haven Police haven't a clue as to who might have done this horrible thing. I myself have hired two separate private investigators, neither of whom has come up with even the remotest possibility of who killed Morgan or why. Both the agencies I employed have staffs and have assured me they are using all available people in the pursuit of the murderous fiend. But I have learned through sources, that during these financial hard times they are more interested in paying their bills than doing their job."

He certainly had a dignified air about him. But there was no hiding the great pain this man was obviously attempting to conceal. I had learned long ago never to say anything until the clients told their whole story. Even though I already knew I couldn't do anything to help this man, I felt I should listen if for no other reason than out of respect.

His deep blue eyes stared directly into mine. "Mr. Conte, my only son has been viciously slain. My wife and I mourn beyond anyone's conception. She has become almost completely insane with grief. It has been very difficult for us to even be in the same room together for too long because we constantly remind each other of our pain. There is one thing, though, that we both speak of everyday—and that is our son's killer. We want him found. We want him brought to justice. We want to see him and contribute to his suffering."

He stopped talking long enough to light up another Camel. This was going to be a difficult situation. How was I going to tell this sorrowful man that even though I was a private investigator, I was similar to a licensed lawyer who chases ambulances.

He was very impressive. I could see him obviously wrestling with his pain, all the time keeping his dignity in tact.

"I have come here, Mr. Conte, after finding out a great deal about you, in the hope that you will be able to help Mrs. Barnes and myself."

For a moment I squirmed in my swivel chair thinking back to Gina—*sodomita mi*—holy jeez. I cleared my throat, "Mr. Barnes, indeed if you have looked into my history as a private investigator you must certainly realize I have never done any significant criminal work, especially of this magnitude. I work almost exclusively for insurance companies and divorce lawyers. I would truly like to help you, but I'm afraid all I can do is recommend yet another private investigative agency that might do a better job than the previous two."

He stubbed out his Camel in the ashtray and leaning forward, offered me an imposing glare. "No, Mr. Conte. I do have the right man in you. You have no idea how highly recommended you come. Are you familiar with a Mr. Calvin Thornbuckle?"

THE FOURTH ESTATE MURDERS

"No, I'm afraid not."

"Well then, Mutual Trust Insurance Company out of Hartford?"

"Why yes, of course. I do a lot of their injury claims work."

"You should know that Calvin Thornbuckle is the president of Mutual Trust. This company also insures my factory here in Bridgeport. Mr. Thornbuckle tells me his agents claim you are, by far the best investigator the company has ever employed. It seems you have many police connections, especially here in Bridgeport. And it was here to this dreary city that my son had been coming every night for a week before his murder."

Jeez I didn't realize they thought so much of me at Mutual Trust; if I had known, I would have charged them more money. I stuck my arms out in a helpless gesture, not wanting to lead this gentleman on for a single moment. "This is way out of my league, Mr. Barnes. It would be a waste of my time and your money for me to take on this case."

He was by no means excepting my response, "I told you I hired two private investigators—the second I employed also to scrutinize your situation. I know that you're divorced with two daughters and you pay the mortgage on your ex-wife's house, plus child support. Your income tax shows that you make less than six hundred dollars a week and that is why you probably reside in this flea-bitten office of yours. I also know that you were the best man at Tom Harrington's wedding. He is the desk sergeant at the Bridgeport Police Station and, I'm told, one of the only honest cops on the force. That's why he's behind the desk. But he's not entirely honest, is he? He passes on police information to you whenever you need it; for this you pay him part of your fee. If any of this information is incorrect, then please except my apology."

I returned his knowing gaze, "Naw, you pretty much got it right. But none of what you said means I'm capable of finding a murderer."

"No, I know this Mr. Conte, but I have no trust whatsoever in the police. In the past week or so I've concluded that you're my only hope. You see, Mr. Conte, I also knew your dad. I know where you come from. Many years ago your father was a production manager at Sikorsky Aircraft; I spent over a week trying to hire him away from Sikorsky's. My factory was, at the time, having great difficulty on the production line. As you know, I was unsucessful, your father having chosen to remain loyal to Sikorsky. Nevertheless we parted genially, with him suggesting a production procedure I still use to this day."

My head began to whirl. This is what I had originally set out to do, way back when Tommy and I had entered the Police Academy together. All I wanted was to become a cop for a year or two, then become a serious private investigator. But I never even got out of the academy. Thoughts were shooting through my head, flirting with ideas, "Mr. Barnes, please call me Jimmy. What makes you think you won't sour on my investigative techniques as you did on the other private eyes?"

His face and overall demeanor seemed to warm up a little, "I don't know, Jim, but I am here to show you in any way I can that I'll put my complete trust in you."

With that statement out of the way, he reached into his inside pocket, pulling out his checkbook. "How does one thousand a week sound? Paid weekly, in advance, by mail. With a bonus of one hundred thousand dollars paid when you find the bastard who killed my Morgan. I will sign a contract to that effect."

How could I refuse? "I will not only need a contract to show that I am employed by you. I will also want my first weeks check paid now in advance, plus another check for five thousand which you can deduct from the one hundred thousand dollar bonus, if I earn it. This is going to take time and money. I have found that the only thing for free is the air; both good and bad information cost money."

He pulled out his pen, "Then you will do it?"

"Yes, I will try. I'll turn over the little work I have now to another investigator and work solely on this case. I must tell you though that part of that five thousand advance will go for clothes for my daughters and to pay for a few back mortgage payments on my wife's house, and maybe a few in advance."

He had already begun writing out the checks, "Do whatever is necessary. Just find whomever it was that took my son's life'"

Before Mr. Barnes left me, he gave me all the information he could about his son's death. The autopsy with postmortem papers, and newspaper clippings—which were many because Morgan Barnes was a journalist for the New Haven Register, one of Connecticut's finest newspapers. The police report offered nothing much except "cause of death: strangulation". There was one thing that sent a chill through me as I read the articles of Morgan's murder, the killer had left a note:

> *Why do I feel you should die?*
> *Two clues. No more lies.*
> *What you said with your last breath*
> *brought it on . . . death, death, death.*

The building my office was in had three floors, two of which had apartments and offices, with five stores on the street level including a bar called the Stayawhile Tavern. It was an unusual bar because it only had a license to sell beer and wine —hard liquor was not allowed; but there were always a few bottles hidden behind the bar. The patrons were mostly retired or on the verge of retirement; however, there was a small group of cops and a few wayward gamblers that hung around there, too. I ate most of my meals there because it was so cheap and convenient, and since I didn't have a set in my office, it was also a place to watch television. They never played music in the Stayawhile, but the T.V. could always be heard in the background. The decor was a nicotine brown from years of cigar and cigarette smoke. And the customers—they hated everyone, including each other.

The owner of the Stayawhile was a Greek named Georgie who also didn't find many nice things to say about anyone, but he reserved his most prejudiced animosity for himself. At this time his face was all singed and blistered from sticking his head inside his kitchen oven, turning the gas on to its fullest, and breathing in the lethal fumes with the idea of ending his existence. Unfortunately for Georgie, he forgot to extinguish the pilot light in the greasy old oven and gave his face a terrible charring.

I entered the Stayawhile already knowing it was too early for Tommy to show up, but he'd stop in for a beer or two after his shift. He always did. I hadn't been inside but a minute when Georgie yelled to me from behind the bar, "Look-it dee television, Jimmy, we're killing all de towelheads."

Scotty, the local mailman who had already finished his route, joined in, "Aye, this war will be over in a few more days. These sandworm Arabs can't last much longer."

I yelled over all the noise, "Georgie, give me a meatball grinder and a cold beer."

"Comin' up, Jimmy."

Three of the old-timers needed a fourth for airplane pinochle. They asked me to join in but I politely refused, instead taking my beer to a booth nearest the television. The all-news station, CNN, was showing clips of the precision bombing being executed by the American and British pilots on ammo dumps, chemical factories and the like. It was incredible. They could guide these smart missiles directly into a smokestack. Anytime they'd show a clip of this, it would bring forth a raucous response from the Staya-while crew.

Georgie brought over the meatball grinder. I hoped none of the dry skin shedding from his face had fallen onto my sandwich. "Hey, Jimmy, I go down to Fat Mike's to shoot crap tonight after I close. You wanna come along?"

"No thanks, Georgie. I have a lot of work to do. Maybe some other time."

"Yeah sure, Jimmy. A lot of work. What you do, work on some poor woman body? 'Cause that dee only work I ever see you do at night."

From behind Georgie the familiar voice joined in, "No, Georgie, at night he also figures out how he can make his mortgage payments."

Georgie turned around smiling, "Hey, Tommy, sit down, sit down. I get you beer."

"How are you doing, Tom?"

"Okay, Jimmy. Except Sally called me again today. She said you haven't given the mortgage company any money yet. She's worried they might start foreclosure proceedings on the house."

"Why does she always have to call you, Tommy? What does she expect, you to make the payments?"

"We're friends, Jimmy. That's all."

"Yeah, I know. You're the one she should have married."

Tommy's Irish face turned red anytime he showed the slightest emotion. "Why's that, Jimmy? Because we would have been good for each other or you wouldn't have to be paying all this money every month?"

"Will you be quiet and listen. I got real good news."

Georgie was coming over and I didn't want to say anything in front of the crazy Greek. He set the beer down and asked, "What else, guys?"

"I'll tell you what else, Georgie, bring me and my best man here a shot of that Irish whiskey you got hidden under the bar and give everyone else a beer."

Georgie walked off impressed. I took a bite out of my grinder while Tommy studied me. "What's going on, Jimmy, something is strange here."

"We took on a new client today, Tom."

Tom Harrington was like a brother to me. We grew up in the same neighborhood—me with two sisters and Tommy with four. Neither one of us had a brother, so we always kind of thought of each other as a brother. We were each other's best man at our weddings. Just like our fathers before us, we made mostly all girls; I had two daughters and Tommy had five. The only difference was that he was still married to his wife, Alice, while mine had divorced me almost two years ago. Everyone liked Tommy, especially all the other cops. He never took a bribe, not even at Christmastime. The only way he made extra money was by getting information for me. No one seemed to mind his doing this one thing. After all he had seven mouths to feed, including his own.

I told Tommy the whole story about Remsen Barnes' visit, the money he was paying and the bonus he offered if we found the culprit. Tommy excitedly gulped down his Irish whiskey and asked, "Can you do it, Jimmy?"

"Do what?"

"Find the killer?"

"I don't know, Tom, but I can tell you this, I can't do it without your help."

Tommy smiled, "We're going to finally make some real money, aren't we?"

"I'll say, if we can find the bastard or bastards who killed Morgan Barnes, we'll both be able to pay off our mortgages and have a little left over."

Tommy's smile broadened, "Let's go shoot some hoops before it gets too dark."

"Naw, I got a date."

"You and that dick of yours. You better watch out, someday you may put it in the wrong place."

I laughed, "You should have seen where I almost put it today."

Tommy had friends in the police departments all over the state. I told him I'd have five hundred in cash for him tomorrow and to use it, if he had to, to pay for any information about the Morgan Barnes murder. He said he knew one of the daytime desk sergeants in the New Haven police. He claimed that by tomorrow night we'd be up-to-date on what the police had on the murder. He rose to leave, but before he went he asked, "Do me a favor? Go and see Sally before you go out tonight."

"Jeez, Tommy. Isn't it bad enough she pushes me around. Don't let her con you."

"Will you go see her?"

"Yeah, I'll go see her."

Everytime I left the Stayawhile it seemed I had to reajust my vision. In the tavern, everything was brown or had a brown tint. Lately bikers had started hanging around the neighborhood. As my eyes grew accustomed to the light, I saw one sitting astride his bike seemingly looking for trouble. Scotty claimed the only reason they started hanging around the Northend was because they were afraid to go to any other parts of Bridgeport. And these days I couldn't blame them.

I drove up Main Street toward Trumbull. As I drove further north, the smog cloud gradually thinned out. This was Bridgeport, the "Park City". When I was a kid we were all proud of our industrial city. All our parents worked in factories. It was blue collar, but a darn good place to live. Now it was filthy and corrupt. Seventy-five percent of the city was on some kind of welfare. The projects were full of blacks and Puerto Ricans. To most long-time residents of Bridgeport, it didn't matter whether these were good or bad people, what mattered was that most were relocated—state welfare families from the other major Connecticut cities.

It used to be a beautiful city, now it wasn't much better than a nuclear dumpsite. We—the Blacks, Puerto Ricans, Italians, Irish, Poles and Jews—were the lowlifes in the eyes of the rest of the state. Hell, the bones of our main celebrity, "Tom Thumb", the midget of P.T. Barumn fame, were dug up from the cemetery and held for ransom. Many of the people I grew up with had left. Those who stayed were like myself, prisoners of Bridgeport for one reason or another.

I pulled into the driveway of what used to be my home, located on the town line of Bridgeport and Trumbull. Before I even got to the front door, Sally was out to greet me. "I thought we had agreed, Jim. You wouldn't come here without calling first."

"That's right, Sally, and you were supposed to stop calling Tommy and crying on his shoulder."

"You haven't made a mortgage payment in two months. What was I supposed to do?"

"I'll pay them tomorrow and give them two months in advance."

I started to walk inside the house, but she moved in front of me. "Jim, wait a minute, we have to talk before you go inside. Let's go and sit in your Wagoneer for a few moments."

"Is something wrong with Jeanie or Sara?"

"No, no, Jimmy, just come on. Let's get in your car, I'm cold."

Once we got inside she warmed up almost immediately. She

gave me a long look. "I can smell some woman's scent on you."

"Yeah . . . and so what!"

"Alright, Jimmy, calm down. It's no big thing. I guess if you are going to make four mortgage payments tomorrow you made some decent money lately."

"Yes. Sometime before you get off work tomorrow, I'll stop at the health food store and give you some cash for new clothes for the girls."

"Good, they certainly can use some."

"Can I go in and see them now?"

"They're not home, Jim."

"Then why are we talking in the car?"

She put her hand on mine, "I have someone with me."

I pulled my hand away yelling, "Don't touch me, you tofu-beanspout-eating bitch! How dare you talk about a woman's scent on me while you got some guy's organic carrot in your mouth."

She looked at me like I wasn't worth the argument and opened the car door, "That's all, no more, good-bye. I don't want to hear anymore of your vulgar insults."

Before she could get out of the car, I rallied and dismissed my jealously, "Hey Sally, you're still looking great."

She had always been easy prey for a compliment. She began to regain her composure. "No, Jimmy, it's you who looks good, and that's one of your curses—that along with that wild cowboy between your legs."

Sally and I used to say to each other that she was smarter than me and I was better in bed than her, but I always thought she was better in bed too. I asked, "Do you think we'll ever do it again?"

"Maybe, but first you have to treat me with some respect, and I don't see that happening in the near future."

I wished I could respect the life she had chosen, but I was too bitter. It was me who had to support her and the girls. I had no time for respect. I moved closer to her. "I'll see you tomorrow at the health food store, Sally. Come here and give me a kiss good-night."

She checked to see if her guest was looking out the front window, then quickly leaned over and gave me a peck. I grabbed her soft boobs for a moment and was about to sink my face into them, but she pulled away. I gave her my best smile, "Give my two little girls a kiss good-night for me."

She smiled, and ran off toward the house. I yelled, "Stay away from those organic carrots."

TWO

Paul Nelson was just returning on his Yamaha 750. He pulled into the Oak Tree Trailer Park, fifteen miles west of Bridgeport, in the city of Southport. He had been here just over four months, yet he had already become very popular with the residents who lived near his camper. But he was a very special favorite of Mrs. Herman, the owner of the trailer park. Blanche Herman had been watching the entrance of the park, waiting patiently for Paul Nelson to return. As soon as she saw him pull in, she grabbed the plate of freshly-baked, chocolate chip cookies and hurried off to greet him. He had just pulled his bag of groceries, with the Bridgeport Post sticking out the top, from the carry basket at the rear of the Yamaha.

He saw her approaching with the plate and quickly prepared himself. He was not only adept at disguise, but also at mood change. Mrs. Herman practically sang out her words, "Oh, Mr. Nelson. Good evening, isn't it just a wonderful evening?"

Paul Nelson spoke in the voice he used since he had arrived at the trailer park, "Ah, yes, Mrs. Herman, it is a lovely evening and nothing brightens it more than your wonderful smile."

"Mr. Nelson, you do know how to flatter a lady. I've made a batch of chocolate chip cookies as a bribe in the hope that you'll except my offer to help run the trailer park."

"But Mrs. Herman . . . Blanche—I have to go to Hartford shortly and I can't say when I'll be returning."

She grinned, "Then that means you will be back, yes?"

He returned her smile, "Yes, Blanche, I will be back."

After a little more conversation, he entered his camper. He put his groceries away, sat down with a glass of milk and some of Blanche Herman's cookies, and opened the Bridgeport Post. The newspaper was becoming an ever-increasing problem for Paul Nelson. News hurt and bad news really hurt—but lies? Well, lies by journalists for the sake of making their columns more interesting was simply too much for Paul Nelson. He began flipping the pages, angrily shoving the chocolate chip cookies into his mouth, one after the other. Then he started crinkling the pages, but not before his ever-watchful eyes had seen all the words. Outwardly he spoke and presented himself in many different ways, but inwardly the voice with which he spoke to himself was always the same. A slow, deep whisper accompanied by a sibilant ess.

He stopped flipping the pages and spread the newspaper out flat across the table. There it was, an article by James Walblont entitled, "Looking at Iraq with Peter Arnett". *'Itsss him again.'* The article continued, "Peter Arnett, the gifted reporter who won the Pulitzer Prize in 1966, is at it again giving us an inside look at Iraq as only he can." *'What about Viet Nam?'* "Mr. Arnett, who looks fit and even robust, has once again shown his willingness to go where many other journalists are reluctant to go." *'How about our guyss? The onesss he betrayed.'* "Senator Alan Simpson, a Wyoming Republican, has called Peter Arnett a sympathizer with Iraq. And has gone on to say that he was also a sympathizer with the Viet Cong during the Viet Nam War." *'Yess, betraying our boysss. Maybe he ssshould've brought the Iraqisss ssome weaponss when he paid hiss call.'*

For the past month Paul Nelson had read every viewpoint presented by James Walblont. It wasn't just this one article, but rather the combination of the past months' editorials that had sent him into a rage. James Walblont always made a point of

THE FOURTH ESTATE MURDERS

smearing Pentagon officials while praising his fellow journalists. It wasn't only Walblont, it was all journalists that got under his skin. But Walblont was so self-serving, such an ass-kisser that this reader could simply take no more. And crumpling the page hissed, '*Die, Walblont, die. . . .*'

The thing I hated most about waking up in my office was not seeing my two little girls anymore. It had been two years, yet I still couldn't get out of my memory the feeling of them jumping onto my bed to wake me up. They were growing up now and beginning to think about boys. I wondered if they still loved me as much as I loved them.

Outside I could hear the roar of a motorcycle. Why was it necessary for them to rev their engines so much? If bikers were so interested in being noticed, why the hell didn't they just wear pink shirts and green plaid pants like golfers do?

I shook my head, trying to clear up the last of this lingering dream I'd been having the last week or more. I had to get up and get ready. A very busy day was in store for me. I was going to have to start organizing myself. The first thing I thought about doing was getting rid of all my baseball trophies and Hopalong Cassidy books. They were everywhere in the little bedroom. I knew after Sally brought them all over here I should have thrown them out or given them away, but even though I was pushing forty, I still wasn't entirely convinced that I couldn't catch on with a major league baseball team. Those used to be Tommy's and my goals. Tommy was going to be a pro basketball player and I was going to be a left-handed hitting, center fielder? Unfortunately for Tommy, he never grew any taller after he reached five feet nine, besides he was way too slow. Yeah, well, I did make it to almost six feet, but my problem was that I went to the Woodstock Concert. After Woodstock it must have been four or five years before I even thought about baseball again.

Then there were all my Hoppy books. I spent a good part of my childhood reading them. I loved Hopalong Cassidy. When I finally reached puberty, my sisters used to joke that if anyone was looking for me I was probably playing with Hoppy. Little did they know how right they were.

I spent a good part of the day in my office reading the newspaper articles regarding Morgan Barnes' murder. I got the feeling from the stories and the police preliminary report that he knew the person who killed him. His wallet was taken, along with his watch and ring, yet something made me think he knew who it was. Before I even went to the New Haven Long Wharf where the slaying took place, I first wanted to see what Tommy had dug up for me.

After I read all I could absorb for one day, I took a pistol permit application out of my desk drawer. For twelve years now I'd picked up applications for gun permits but was always too lazy or disinterested to fill one out. If I was going to find this killer, I sure as hell should get myself a weapon in addition to my tired old fists.

I didn't get out of my office until afternoon. I think it was the first time since Sally and I split up that I was able to stay there that long alone during the daytime. I deposited the money Remsen Barnes had given me into my own checking account and immediately took the weight of my heavy bills off my mind. I took out two thousand in cash. I dropped off five hundred dollars at the Green Earth Health Food Store where Sally worked; I wanted to give Tommy some cash he'd need, and the rest was for me.

The first thing I noticed when I entered the Stayawhile was a few of the bikers having beers in the corner booth. I don't know why, but this bothered me. I walked straight back to the other end of the bar and into the open kitchen where Georgie was preparing a few grinders. "Hey, Jimmy, how you do, boy?"

"Okay, Georgie. What's going on with those bikers?"

"Nothing, they just want to eat. These two sausage grinders for them."

The dry, peeling, scaled skin dropped freely off of Georgie's face. He was getting up there in age. Many years ago he'd spent some time in a Turkish prisoner-of-war camp. He supposedly wrote a book about it. He claimed a lot of things, like he hasn't washed his hair in forty years—instead he combs it through every morning. He said he learned that in prison.

Georgie was the only worker in the Stayawhile except for some of his customers who would get their own beers when he was too busy. He handed me the two plates. "Here, Jimmy, be good kid and bring dese grinders over to de motorcycle guys." He handed them to me and scooted behind the bar to the welcoming insults of patrons with empty beer glasses.

I walked over to the two bikers and deposited a plate in front of each one. Both men were completely attired in leather, chains, whiskers and tatoos. They briefly looked my way. I gave neither a chance to speak. "Let me ask you something? Why the hell do you have to make so much goddamn noise with your motorcycles?"

They smiled at each other. They were so cool. One took a bite out of his grinder then said, "I'll tell ya, man. It's 'cause we know it annoys ya faggots so fuckin' much."

"Oh yeah. The only queers around here are you piston-sucking low-lifes."

The one with the leather jacket, chains and an earring started to get up. I pushed him back down in the booth, saying, "Sit down, you fat sack of shit."

That gesture only brought them both up at me. What had I

done? I back-peddled toward the bar. The one without the earring took a swing at me, which brought everybody off their bar stools. I countered with an errant swing of my own. Georgie came running out from the kitchen with a butcher knife. Right around this time Tommy walked through the front door with Ivan King, a homicide detective with the Bridgeport police. Tommy stuck his foot between the legs of the earringed one who got tangled up and fell. Ivan King, who was dressed in street clothes, pulled out his .45 and stuck it in the face of the one without the earring. "C'mon baby, let me improve that ugly face of yours with a few hollow points."

The biker put his hands up in the surrender position while the other picked himself up off the floor. The one with the earring barked, "We ain't lookin' fer no trouble . . ." and backed his way to the door. The other grabbed the two sausage grinders as they retreated out the exit.

Tommy was all smiles, "Could this be the return of the old Wild Man Jim?"

Georgie laughed, "Yes, Tommy. I think so. I see it all. Jimmy he looking to kick ass."

"Please, don't start on me. I'm just tired of being woken up all the time by their revving engines," I shouted.

Ivan King, eager for battle, bellowed, "Let's go out there and chase'um the fuck outta here."

Everyone in Bridgeport called Detective King "Ivan the Terrible". He was a bad-ass I really didn't care for. But Tommy didn't agree, often insisting that he was a good man. I yelled, "We aren't going anywhere."

"Who the fuck died and left Conte in charge?"

Tommy got between us, "Georgie, get us three beers. Come on, let's go sit down. We're on the same freakin' team."

Ivan gave me his crazy-man smile. What could I do? I

THE FOURTH ESTATE MURDERS

returned it with a submissive one.

Soon after Georgie brought the beers, I went into the men's room to clean myself up. Less than a minute later Tommy joined me. "Wild Man, it looked like the ole days out there."

"Forget it, Tom, it was my fault and I'm sorry I even said anything to the bikers. Why the hell did you have to bring Ivan the Terrible here? I figured you'd realize how serious the Morgan Barnes investigation is."

"Jimmy, I'm way ahead of you. Ivan's working with the New Haven police. The word out of New Haven is they think the killer came from Bridgeport."

I showed Tommy a look of delight. "Alright Tom! Did you mention anything to Ivan?"

"No, I don't want him to catch on. That's why I brought him here. Don't let him know what we're up to. Let's have a few beers with him and see what we can find out."

"Well, let's not be impolite and keep Officer King waiting."

Ivan had already finished half his beer by the time Tommy and I returned.

"Hey, King, I'm sorry about the misunderstanding. I have no desire to get into a fight with a few bikers."

"Yeah, I figured that. Tommy told me you've turned into a first class wimp."

I looked over at Tommy who was trying to hide his sheepish smile. "Alright, let's forget it. Come on, let me buy you another beer?"

When I returned with his beer, I could overhear them discussing the Iraqi war. I jumped right in, "Eh, this war sucks. Believe it or not, I'm on a case directly related to the war."

Tommy asked, "What the hell are you doing, Jimmy?"

I looked at them both cautiously and dictated, "This can't leave this table." Both nodded. "I'm doing a job for Barnes' Girdle and

Bra. They've lost sixteen reservists to this Iraqi thing. Most were in management. The company is being robbed blind by their replacements. Shit, I was just up in their executive offices yesterday. The main man, Remsen Barnes, looked a mess. I can't believe he's letting something like this get to him so badly."

Ivan was in such a hurry to respond that he abruptly pulled the beer bottle away from his mouth causing it to foam out of the neck.

"Jimmy, that's why you didn't make it at the police academy. You were never able to understand the fuckin' overall picture. The guy's hurting—not over a few bucks, but because somebody took out his fuckin' kid."

"Yeah . . . yeah . . . that's right his son died."

"Died! You stupid fuck, he was murdered. Some fuckin' spade put his lights out."

"A black guy?"

"Yeah, that's right, a fuckin' porch monkey."

Tommy asked, "How do you know it was a black guy, I-Man? I thought this was a New Haven thing?"

"It is, Tom, but Supt. Finnigan put Jenkins and myself on the case to work with New Haven. We think the boon who killed the Barnes kid is from Bridgeport."

I asked, "How do you know he's black?"

"'Cause they found some negro hair on the deceased. We're pretty sure it's a male because they got footprints of sneakers size twelve or thirteen. We got some other information that corraborates that it's a man."

I asked, "What?"

But Tommy jumped in, "That's classified, isn't it, I-Man?"

Ivan looked confused, "What's the matter, Tom, you don't trust your friend?"

I answered for Tommy, "No, Ivan, that's not it. It's just none of my business, and to tell you the truth I don't really want to know."

We had a few more beers until Ivan finally left. Tommy made it clear that he could handle Ivan from here on out. I gave him a few hundred in cash and my pistol permit application. He said that with a few bucks he might be able to get through the red tape in a short time and get me what he agreed was necessary for a legal gun.

Tommy was a stereo-typical Irish-American: plump, red-freckled face, and a short fuse; pretty much an all-around smart kind of guy. He used many different techniques in dealing with various people. But with me it was always the same—abruptly honest and, most of the time, caring. He had such a large family to feed that what he said next didn't surprise me. "You know, that fucking jerk Ivan is a pretty good investigator."

"Yeah, so?"

"Yeah, so shit, Jimmy, what if he or some other homicide detective finds the killer before we do? No one hundred thousand dollars."

"Yes, so that's the breaks, isn't it?"

"No, Jimmy. You got to get your ass out there and find this black dude before he does."

"Don't worry, we'll get him."

"Oh yeah, why's that?"

I gave him my most charming smile. "Because, Tom, haven't we always been on the first team?"

He loved it when I talked like this. "Whaaa-hoo, let's have a taste of Georgie's whiskey!"

THREE

His mouth tightened while he watched the cable news station. There was Peter Arnett offering his sympathetic viewpoint over and over again on the Iraqi government's position. If there was only some way for Paul to get to Baghdad, he could silence forever the subversive, left-wing comrade, Peter Arnett.

Paul Nelson had spent a good part of his life involved in every aspect of the stage: actor, director, stage hand and makeup artist, at which he was very good. Having gone to various drama schools, he worked for a number of years in small theater groups. He played every role he had ever had to its maximal. Yet he had never landed a significant part with anything other than small companies. Shakespeare was his favorite playwright and The Tragedy of King Richard the Third, his favorite play. But Othello, the Moor of Venice was his best role. His most memorable part had been way back in the early seventies and it was that certain character he played with which he identified the most. A group of out-of-work actors got together in Boston and presented J.R.R. Tolkien's "The Hobbit". As good as the rendition was, it failed completely. The character Paul Nelson portrayed in the production was a young lad named Smegal who killed another boy out of greed. Later in the production Smegal turns into the black, slithering, subterranean named Gollum, who hissed when he spoke. It wasn't long after the failure of The Hobbit that Paul Nelson committed his first murder. He killed always in disguise and, in the beginning, only for money. Now, the money hardly meant anything. Acting was all of it. Suburbia and the cities were his stage and any who crossed his path, the audience. The victims were his *coups de theatre.*

There were times when he wished to share his success with everyone. He even left clues. Most were given to throw any pursuers off the right track. But he always tried to leave one or two indirect hints to any who might dare to go beyond normalcy to divergency. He still, at times, played who he really was, but only when it was absolutely necessary.

All his clothes were bought at second hand stores or yard sales. He always ripped the labels out and even dyed most of the articles of clothing. Sometimes he'd turn long sleeved shirts into short sleeved ones. He would do whatever it took to make sure his clothes, or anything else, was non-traceable to himself.

At four o'clock in the morning while it was still dark, Paul Nelson, disguised as a Puerto Rican by wearing a slicked-down, black hair piece, walked his Yamaha out of the trailer park and drove to the Bridgeport Post building. When the sun rose up over the polluted Long Island Sound, he drove through the Post's parking lot hoping to find the parking space with James Walblont's name on it. But the numbered spaces only read "reserved", so he spent the next few hours surveying the whole block on which the Bridgeport Post stood.

At ten o'clock when it seemed certain all the employees had entered the building, so did Paul Nelson. He sauntered up to the reception desk like he was moving to a Latin beat. He tapped his knuckles on the receptionist's telephone. The young, saucy blond behind the desk looked up, a little annoyed, "Yes, can I help you?"

"Como esta, Senorita? Si, yes. Me hav de message for El Senor Yames Walblont."

The attractive blond asked, "Do you mean James Walblont?"

"Si, si. Donde? Where he at?"

She put her hand out, "Give it to me. I'll see that he gets it."

"Oh, no, I cannot do that, Senorita, de message eets personal. Mi jefe say for Yames Walblont, solomente."

She smiled, unable to help herself, amused by the Puerto Rican who seemed to have jumping beans inside his pants. "Take the elevator to the fourth floor, turn right and walk to the end of the hallway. Just ask anyone there and they'll show you the way to his desk."

"Much thank you, Senorita."

The fourth floor was like the usual hectic newsroom. A passerby directed the Puerto Rican to James Walblont's desk. It was amid many other desks that were back-to-back with one another. The Puerto Rican tapped on James Walblont's desk. Walblont looked up, vexed. "Yes, what is it?"

"Perdona me, Senor. I hav dis muy big envelope for you."

"Okay, thank you, put it down, please. I'll get to it as soon as I can."

Doing as the reporter said, he placed the envelope on the desk, stepped back and watched until Walblont looked up, still irritated. "Well, is there anything else? What are you waiting for?"

The Puerto Rican stuck out his hand, "De tip, Senor."

The woman who had the desk adjacent to Walblont's, chuckled, but not so with the annoyed reporter who asked her, "Lesile. Do you have any change or anything? The smallest bill I have is a twenty."

"Sure, what do you want me to give him, Jim?"

"Give him fifty cents or something like that."

Lesile laughed, "Oh, you're a real big spender." She reached inside her purse and handed the Latin messenger two one dollar bills.

"Mil gracias, Senorita. Maybe you like to help me espend eet, huh?"

James Walblont was quick to break in, "Okay, Jose, this isn't a Latin disco. We have work to do so if you don't mind."

'Yesss, but I do mind.' He turned quickly and disappeared.

The reporter opened the envelope only to find another that said—IMPORTANT, PLEASE OPEN VERY CARE-FULLY—The next envelope was sealed so many different ways that it took him a minute or so to open it. It read:

> *I've read so much of what you've written,*
> *That it sets my mind afire.*
> *I read too much of what you've written,*
> *Telling me you stand by the liar.*
>
> *Arnett was in the north while our boys died.*
> *Dancing with the enemy while the mothers cried.*
> *You have until tomorrow to unsay what's been said.*
> *Or join the other that I've made dead.*

James Walblont stuck the note under his desk blotter then hurried out to see if he could intercept the Latin messenger before he exited the building. The Puerto Rican was nowhere to be found. . . .

Later at the end of the business day, Paul Nelson watched as James Walblont walked into the parking lot and got into a blue Chevy. Now that the reporter's car had been identified, there was no reason to hang around the Post building any longer. He rode off on his Yamaha, but not to go to the Oak Tree Trailer Park. There were other people to see. Yes, others who had roles in his far-reaching plot. As the director, it was necessary for him to make sure they were rehearsing their parts, all-be-it unwittingly.

When he was far enough away from the Post building, he threw the Latin costume into three separate trash cans. The part he had played as the Puerto Rican was over. He was pleased with his performance. Someday, Paul Nelson was sure, his work would become famous. Drama teachers might outwardly criticize his psychopathic methods, but in time they'd have no choice but to admire what he had done and eventually introduce his techniques into their teachings. For now though, he would have to content himself with the overall production. He steered his Yamaha towards St. Mary's by the Sea where Mr. and Mrs. Remsen Barnes resided.

FOUR

Ever since I broke up with Sally, I've searched for another woman like her. Not that she was all-understanding or the ideal wife, because she wasn't. Nevertheless I loved her and I loved women like her. The smart, independent type. The kind you could never control.

Too bad Hoppy wasn't as discriminating in looking for love. Hoppy could find something attractive in every woman. A subtle curve, an intoxicating perfume, clothes designed for seduction, even a cigarette dangling from the right lady's mouth. There was even something appealing about women who preferred other women. . . .

I got off the Connecticut Turnpike at Exit 46. I had acquired loads of information and descriptions on where—and possibly how—the murder of Morgan Barnes had taken place. I drove my Wagoneer on down to the New Haven Long Wharf. The car radio was offering an account of the air war going on over the skies of Iraq. I shut it off, preferring silence and the prevailing aura of death that surrounded the area. There were a few vendors pushing Jenny's Famous Hot Dogs carts. It was chilly, causing steam to rise from the carts.

I had papers and photographs laying out all over the passenger seat. I pulled the Wagoneer over when I came to the telephone pole with the number tag "15" on it.

I walked on a sidewalk atop a four foot high seawall. I

counted the correct number of steps from telephone pole 15 and found myself at the spot where the murder had taken place. I jumped off the seawall onto the mixed rock and sand shore. This was where it had happened. The only man-made noises were from a foghorn on a lighthouse way out in the harbor and the far-off cars swishing by on the turnpike.

What a spot for a murder. Absolutely no place to hide. The telephone poles had streetlights on them which meant the area was lit up at night. I scanned the beach hoping I might find something the police had overlooked, but almost four months had passed since the murder.

I glanced across the skyline off to the east where there was a large restaurant, and then to the north with the skyscrapers of New Haven. Below them was the turnpike and a few billboards in between. One said "Cranston Chocolates, HOW SWEET IT IS." The other offered, "This spring at the Shakespearean Theatre: KING LEAR, RICHARD THE THIRD AND OTHEL-LO . . . Information available at all Ticketrons."

There were no clues but I still didn't consider it a waste of time. I learned a long time ago that in any type of investigation you ride your hunches out. Just by looking at this eerie place I had become pretty sure the deceased had known the person who had killed him.

Morgan Barnes had been doing a series of articles on the slums of Bridgeport for the New Haven Register. Whenever there was a lull in the local news in Connecticut, someone would write about Bridgeport. I think it gave the rest of the state the opportunity to pat themselves on the back: "Look at those lowlifes. How can they live under those conditions? The whole city stinks. The armpit of the state." Nobody, absolutely nobody likes Bridgeport, including those of us who inhabit it.

I paid a visit to the New Haven Library and began thumbing

THE FOURTH ESTATE MURDERS

my way through back issues of the New Haven Register, looking for any articles written by Morgan Barnes. After a while I realized his column only appeared on Tuesdays and Fridays. He certainly had been writing about Bridgeport slums. He did four separate features on just one tenement building on East Main Street. It was all good reading stuff: rats biting children, a cellar used as a refuse dump, people burning fires in empty fifty gallon metal drums inside their apartments for their only source of heat. The building was owned by Jenny's Famous Hot Dogs, Inc.

On the way back to Bridgeport I stopped at my brother-in-law Frankie's restaurant in Milford. He was my good brother-in-law who was married to my good sister, Mary. It was only about an hour before the lunch rush but Frankie, who always worked very hard, still had time for me. At six feet four inches and weighing in at two fifty, he presented an intimidating figure. Nonetheless he was as gentle as a manatee. His eyes lit up when he saw me. "Jimmy, how the hell are you? Where have you been? Mary asks about you all the time. She's worried about you, Jim."

"Aah, Frank, do me a favor and tell her not to worry."

"I do, Jimmy, but you know Mary." Frankie turned around and yelled, "Romeo, bring my brother-in-law a plate of fried calamari."

"No, no food, Frankie. I got work to do."

"Okay, but you're going to do it with some food in your stomach."

That was his way, warm and generous. He gave me a serious look. "Hey, Jimmy, what's on your mind? You look kind of funny."

"It's this case I'm working on, Frank. That's why I stopped here. You being in the food business all your life, I was hoping you might be able to help me."

"Sure, Jimmy, anything. What do you need?"

"Well . . . aah . . . um . . . you have any idea who owns Jenny's Famous Hot Dogs?"

His face changed. I was unable to detect any type of emotion. I got a little nervous. "What's wrong, Frankie?"

"What do you need to know this for?"

"It's the case I'm on, why?"

"Why!? I'll tell you why. It's the mustachios."

"What?"

"You know, the mustaches, the mob."

"Oh shit, really?"

He grimaced, "I'm afraid so, Jimmy."

"Do you know who actually owns it?"

"Yeah, Louie Rosselli."

"Any chance of my talking to him?"

He shook his head, "Not unless you ask Fat Mike first."

"How am I supposed to do that?"

He put his hands out like I was supposed to know the answer. "Lenny! Lenny can get you to see Fat Mike. He comes in for lunch everyday. He'll be here in a little while."

Crazy Lenny was my other brother-in-law. He married my wild sister, Josephine. Lenny did collection work for the mustaches. From Hartford to the New York State line, I knew of no local man more feared.

Frankie and I were munching on the fried calamari, dipping the tasty squid strips in a fresh marinara sauce when Lenny came walking through the door. As soon as he saw me, his usual rugged, menacing expression softened. "Jimmy, where the fuck ya been?"

I got up to greet him. "Hi, Len." That's all I was able to say. He grabbed me in a bear hug and picked me up off the floor. He squeezed me so hard that I emitted a little gas eruption. This pleased Lenny so much that instead of kissing me on the cheek, he bit it, hard. I screamed, "Stop, you crazy bastard, you're hurting me!"

He released his grip and I staggered away holding my bitten cheek. "You're crazy, Lenny, you know that?"

He raised his arms up and half shut his eyes, "Hey, why do ya tink dey call me Crazy Lenny?"

Frankie and Lenny shook hands and the three of us sat down together. Lenny ate the rest of the calamari while he listened to Frankie tell him that I needed to see Fat Mike. Lenny gave me a puzzled look, "What da fuck do ya wanta see him for?"

"I need to ask him if I can talk to Louie Rosselli."

"No fuckin' way. Louie's no good."

"Len, please, it's important."

Frankie jumped in, "Come on, Lenny, he's your brother-in-law."

"Yeah, Len, you wouldn't want Josephine to find out you are seeing Rosalie the meter maid again."

"Ha, ya tell yer sister dat . . . ba-bing, ba-boom, Jimmy. Ya know her. She finds dat out she'll cut my fuckin' balls off. That'll make me one pissed off mudder fucker."

Frankie was an only child so no matter what he always treated Lenny and me like we were his real brothers. "Lenny, Jimmy really needs your help, how can you deny him?"

"Shit, ya know I can't. But dat don't change da fact dat it's gonna cost ya free lunch da rest of da week."

Lenny rode to Bridgeport in the Wagoneer with me. I spent three hours with my two brothers-in-law and neither one ventured to ask me why I needed to question Louie Rosselli. As we approached Bridgeport, the dark smog cloud that hung over the city didn't seem as thick as usual. That was probably because the once-thriving factories of the Fifties, Sixties and Seventies had long since been shut down. It made me wonder why we had any smog at all.

We drove to Housatonic Avenue, just before the Bridgeport docks. One had to be careful driving this street because there were railroad tracks laid all across the road. Most of the buildings were huge, empty, abandoned factories or mills—brick monuments to the glorious blue collar days. In the middle of this industrial specter stood a small bar with two apartments upstairs, the bar was called Fat Mike's.

If you were a hood or a thug in Bridgeport, one way or another you belonged to the fraternity at Fat Mike's. But only mustaches or highly regarded guests made it upstairs to the two apartments. One of the apartments was strictly for gambling, like bookmaking or other on-premises games. The other apartment was Fat Mike's control center where he and his loyal henchmen planned their dirty deeds.

As soon as we walked inside the bar, Phil Ferrelli, someone I had gone to high school with, walked over to greet me. "Hey, Jimmy, where the hell you been?" Instead of shaking my hand he reached to pinch my cheek, the same one Lenny had bitten earlier. As I blocked his hand from doing so, Lenny put his open palm on Phil's face and pushed, "Get da fuck outta here, ya little grease ball."

Phil went toppling backwards. His white patent leather shoes looked like surrender flags waving in the air. I looked at Crazy Lenny, "Why did you have to do that, Len?"

He smiled at me, "Aah, I dunno. I guess it's because he's a fuckin' jerk."

Lenny went upstairs. While I waited, I talked to many old acquaintances. Most wondered what had happened to me. They, having been sheltered all their lives under the arm of Fat Mike or Tony the Lung before him, hadn't realized that I also never

THE FOURTH ESTATE MURDERS

left Bridgeport. Like everyone else, they, too, were interested in the war. Everyone wanted a piece of Saddam Hussein and the so-called pinko commentator for CNN, Peter Arnett.

The men's room in Mike's had a twist. Attached to the urinal was a full-size, cardboard likeness of Saddam with his mouth scissored open. The idea was to try and urinate inside his mouth, if you missed, no problem—it just ran down his military uniform.

Lenny was waiting for me when I returned to the bar area. "Alright, c'mon. Fat Mike will see ya now."

I followed him up the back stairway. Lenny turned to me as we climbed up the narrow steps. "Don't forget, ya treat Fat Mike wid respect."

"What do you want me to do? Kiss his pinky ring?"

"Dat'll do it."

"Yeah, sure, that will be the day."

There were couches and chairs styled right out of the Fifties. But not the espresso machine. It was quite large; imported from Italy. It looked like it was plated with gold and silver.

Fat Mike was just that, very fat. I had known him since I was a kid. He once tried to get Tommy and me to throw a high school basketball game. But he wasn't that bad of a guy, if a thief, murderer, pimp, shylock and drug-dealer is your kind of person. He looked to be in a hurry, pinching my cheek in the same place where Lenny bit it. "Hey, Jimmy, long time no see. Lenny tells me you want to talk to Louie. He's in the other apartment. What the fuck is the matter?"

"Aah, um, I need to know . . . ."

He interrupted before I could say more. "Never mind. You can tell it to Louie 'cause I got to go. Lenny will stay here to make sure you and Louie don't mess the place up. Right, Lenny?"

"Ya got it, Mike."

Fat Mike was gone. He really didn't seem to care what I

wanted to talk to Louie about. In less than five minutes Louie Rosselli barged into the apartment. "All right dis better be real fuckin' good. What the fuck is going on, Lenny?"

Everything about Louie was skinny. His body, his mustache, his nose and, no doubt, his brains. Lenny stood up and thought carefully for a moment; To me that was always the worst possible thing that could happen. "Listen, Lou. First tings first. If ya yell one more fuckin' word, I'll break every fuckin' bone in dat skinny-ass body. Got dat?"

Louie tried to reason as he whispered, "But Lenny, I'm on a roll. I won the last three poker hands, capice?"

"Yeah, capice shit. Answer what my brother-in-law asks ya. Okay, ya skinny wop?"

Louie continued to whisper, "What can I do for you, Jimmy?"

I figured I might as well get right to it. I had no idea how long this interview would last. "Did you know a man by the name of Morgan Barnes?"

Louie jumped up, "What kind of shit is this?"

Lenny helped Louie back into his seat again and then asked me, "Do you know what yer doin', kid?"

"Yes, Len, it's simple. I just have to make sure Louie didn't kill, Morgan Barnes."

Lenny looked overjoyed, "Holy shit, Jimmy, yer finally doin' somethin' wid yer life besides chasin' down some poor bastards for dere alimony checks."

Louie stood up again, "Youse fuckers are crazy. I'm gettin' out of here."

Lenny waved his hands to me in a helpless fashion. "I can't do nuttin' about dis."

I yelled to Louie, "Wait, Lou. You know Lenny here. He'll make sure nothing leaves this room."

He nodded, "What do you want, Jimmy?"

THE FOURTH ESTATE MURDERS

"Did you ice Morgan Barnes?"

"No fuckin' way, but I'll tell you this—I'm glad he's dead. The son-of-a-bitch was giving me so much trouble about one of my apartment buildings that I couldn't have given it away if I wanted to. You know, he was wrong writing articles that Jenny's Hot Dogs were slum lords. Hell, I tried to give that fuckin' building to the state, the city and even to the Feds, nobody wanted it. Naw, I didn't kill him, but I'm glad the scumbag is dead."

I was beginning to think nothing would come of this, then Louie said, "I know who killed him though."

This took me by surprise, "Who, Lou?"

"None of your fuckin' business, asshole!"

Lenny had been looking on, refusing to say anything, having possibly overstepped his bounds. I looked to him for support. "Len, can you help me out here?"

He turned to Louie, "Is da killer one of us?"

Louie shook his head no. Lenny spoke as serious as he could, "Ya tell my brudder-in-law who iced da fag and I'll owe ya one, Lou."

Louie looked at us both, smiled, and sat back down. "You know the kid, Jimmy. Youse used to play ball together."

I tried to gulp, but was unable to swallow, "Who, Lou?"

"You know, that half-white mulinyam. The one that was the quarterback. Juju Sims."

"Juju!?"

"Yeah, the fuckin' spade who thinks he's a white man."

"This is crazy. Why would Juju want to kill Morgan Barnes?"

Louie seemed to enjoy seeing me squirm, "Because he wanted my apartment building. I told him he could have the fuckin' thing for free, before that son-of-a-bitch Barnes forced the city to fine me."

"So what, that doesn't mean Juju would kill him."

"No, huh? The day before Barnes' murder, I told your high-yellow friend that I couldn't stand the pressure anymore and I was gonna have the building condemned. He asked me if there was any way I'd change my mind. I said: 'Get the fuckin' newspaper pest off my back.' The next day Barnes was dead. Two days after that Juju comes around looking for the deed to the building. I tell him to come back in six months when things cool down and it's his."

Louie looked at Lenny. "Now if youse don't mind, I'm outta here. I told your nigger-lovin' brother-in-law all I know. This is going to be one you owe me."

I was speechless. Tommy, Juju and I went all the way back to grammar school. We fought and played against each other all our lives. Juju was the best all-around athlete I'd ever known.

I drove Lenny back to Frankie's restaurant, then spent the rest of the day driving around Bridgeport. It was like my life was passing before me. The city was dying. What had happened? What had gone wrong? We used to be royalty, Bridgeport was our kingdom. We were princes—me, Tommy and some others, like Juju.

FIVE

Paul Nelson, watching the little black and white T.V., saw the coverage of the Allies continued, heavy, air bombardment of the Iraqi forces and civilians. He thought to himself that, if President Bush knew of his extraordinary skills, he could be employed to carry out the assassination of Saddam Hussein. It was blissful thoughts like these that gave him moments of inner peace. It would be a simple matter to take on the identity of a Semite. The costumes would be glorious. A dark shade of makeup would be necessary. The need to "Arabize" would be the same as studying a difficult script, but that would make it more inspirational. Ultimately Saddam would be no match for an actor of such magnitude.

But as well as the war was going, as skilled as the fighting men were, no power in the world could stop the emphasis of the battle from shifting into the hands of the parasitic members of the Fourth Estate. For the past twenty minutes the CNN anchors had been promising their colleague Peter Arnett to their viewers. Now here he was on screen, uncomfortably fidgeting while he spoke of the terrible bombing he and the Iraqi people were taking. His nose looked as if, long ago, some good American's fist had broken it. The viewer was always reminded that his comments were subject to Iraqi censorship and that's how Arnett chose to give America the news.

'I would take him out the sssame day as Husssien, but insstead I will be ssatissfied with Walblont.'

Out of Paul Nelson's refrigerator came three small plastic vials, all containing the toxic venom of the diamondback rattle snake—one of the easiest lethal poisons to procure when in the southwest. The diamondback is a completely helpless, sidewinder creature when crossing a paved road in the middle of a desert. Extracting its venom was another story, but Paul Nelson had become skilled at that procedure.

The minute vials were made out of soft plastic, and corked so none would spill. He pushed through each cork a small syringe— each one placed inside a short, straight length of cylindrical plastic tubing.

He chose for his costume the garb of a city cowboy—not unlike that used by Jon Voight in the movie "Midnight Cowboy". When he would get to this point in his production, he would think many thoughts to himself, always in the tone of a hissing Gollum-like whisper.

At four in the morning, he again quietly wheeled his Yamaha out of the trailer park. He rode into a Bridgeport suburb and waited for the delivery of the morning Bridgeport Telegram, the sister paper to the daily Post. Soon a delivery truck was dropping its bundles in front of the delicatessens and newsstands. He walked up to one such bundle, cut the twine and grabbed a Telegram. He then rode off to an open diner to read the news. He knew Walblont would have a column in today's paper. It wasn't necessary, but he would read it for further motivation.

The diner waitress stood over him watching as he turned the Post's pages in a frenzy, she didn't realize he had no idea she was standing there. *'Where are you, Walblont?'* There it was! This day's title, "THE OTHER ARMY" Subtitled, "OUR BRAVE NEWSPEOPLE, THE OMBUDSMEN OF THE

THE FOURTH ESTATE MURDERS

PERSIAN GULF."

The waitress interrupted, "Ahem, are you gonna have some coffee or what?"

Startled, he looked up at the waitress, but even though he had been caught unawares, he still slipped easily into his role, "Oh purdin me. I sure am sorry, honey gal. Been caught up readin' this here paper o' your'n—fine periodical that it is. Yes, ma'am. I will have some coffee. And give me some o' your eggs and a nice cut o' rare sirloin."

The waitress jotted it down in her little pad and began walking off, only to here the cowboy remind her, "Don't y'all fergit the catsup now, hear???"

He parked his motorcycle a few blocks from the Post building. The city had come alive with morning traffic and pedestrians. He walked as inconspicuously as he could on the street across from the newspaper's parking lot. Finally he saw Walblont's blue Chevy stopped at the traffic light, waiting to make the turn into the parking lot. Paul Nelson placed the first piece of plastic tubing into his mouth with the needle pointing outward. He had cut the length of tubing perfectly. As he walked toward his prey, the only thing sticking out of his mouth was the needle tip too small to detect.

The reporter, after parking the Chevy, was just beginning to stand erect as he got out of his car, when he saw this cowboy-type coming toward him. He had not yet shut his door when the cowboy bit hard on the plastic tubing and the vial inside it, causing the venom to squirt out into the syringe. At close range the cowboy blew hard into the cylinder, ejecting the vial with its deadly poison at needle's end. The first missile caught James Walblont in the neck. The columnist stood stunned for a moment, then reached to pull out the poison dart, unknowingly injecting more of the venom into his body when he squeezed the plastic vial. By this time the cowboy had placed the second plastic cylinder into his mouth, '*Fire two.*'

This dart caught Walblont on his hand as confusion and hysteria began to set in. Now they were only a few feet apart. With the third cylinder already in his mouth, the cowboy took aim at one of Walblont's eyes and nearly bulls-eyed as the missile entered at the upper part of the cheekbone. James Walblont, still alive and very much confused, began to charge his attacker. Paul Nelson reached inside his cowboy jacket and pulled out a knife with a gauze-wrapped handle and stuck it full force into the gut of the dying man. The force of the blow pushed the reporter back inside his Chevy.

Paul Nelson placed the cowboy hat on the head of the dead reporter, took his wallet and watch, then fled for his motorcycle. Before he had made the turn to where he was parked, he had already discarded his cowboy outfit and looked completely different. As quickly as his Yamaha would take him, he moved away from the scene and back to the trailer park. He needed another disguise. There was much to do. This was only Act One. He did not want anyone to get bored. It was necessary to keep the entire audience spellbound.

SIX

After I learned that Juju was our number one and only suspect, I decided to avoid Tommy until I had more information. So I chose instead to talk to Sally and my daughters for a few hours on the phone. They invited me over for dinner the next evening so the girls could model their new clothes for me. I missed them so much.

That morning I woke up from the same, recurrant dream. I was embarrassed to even think about it.

Last night Remsen Barnes had called and left a message on my answering machine asking me to come to his house at two o'clock this afternoon. He said there was no need to confirm if, in fact, I was coming. He stated his address and hung up.

I spent the whole morning going over what I had. Tommy had supplied me with more information than I could possibly go into. All the police procedural red tape was mostly useless. I already believed I was on the right track to finding the killer. Nevertheless I needed to be prepared for my client. I had no desire to get fired, at least not before my next week's paycheck. . . .

St. Mary's by the Sea, was the last wealthy community in Bridgeport. Most of the industrialists had long ago moved their homes away from Bridgeport, choosing the safer, more "white" communities in which to raise their families. But those who had built long ago at St. Marys, still remained—having opted to sink or swim with the rest of the Bridgeportites. Remsen Barnes' Girdle and Bra factory still operated in Bridgeport, he still employed local residents and this is why I believed he still chose to live within the ruins of the once-thriving industrial city.

It was almost impossible to miss the house, sitting as it did on a rise behind a stone wall overlooking Long Island Sound. I pulled the Wagoneer in through the open gate. As I walked up to the front door I couldn't help but notice the beautiful yard and gardens. If it wasn't for the prevailing, distinguishable smell of Bridgeport, one would have thought oneself to be somewhere else.

Remsen Barnes himself answered the door. I had expected some type of servant. "Ah, yes, Mr. Conte. Good of you to come, and promptly, I might add." He showed me the way in with one hand while we shook with his other.

"Good afternoon, Mr. Barnes. What an exquisite home."

"Why, thank you. We like it."

I followed him into a large room probably called a parlor. He pointed to a couch, where I obediently sat, getting my folder of papers prepared for his questions. He looked a little puzzled, "What do you have there, son?"

"Why, aah, well I figured I'd update you on the progress I've made."

"No, that won't be necessary. Not after such a short period of time. I assure you, I was convinced I chose the right man when I came to your office."

I closed my folder. "Well then, I'm a little confused as to exactly why you wished to see me."

"It's not me, it's my wife, Mrs. Barnes. She would like to meet you. I hope you don't mind?"

I squirmed, feeling a little uncomfortable, "No, of course not."

THE FOURTH ESTATE MURDERS

He immediately left the room returning shortly with Mrs. Barnes. She was dressed in what looked to be a very expensive suit. Her gray hair was done up nicely, but she had absolutely no makeup on. Normally that wouldn't be so profound, but in this case it was extremely noticeable. She offered me the slightest smile while her husband introduced us, "Betty, I'd like you to meet Jim Conte. Son, this is my wife Betty Barnes."

She put her hand out and I took it; it was ice cold. "How do you do, Mr. Conte?"

"It's a pleasure to meet you, Mrs. Barnes."

I returned my hand to my side, but the coldness it brought with it ran a chill through my body.

She and her husband sat down on a couch across from mine, I reseated myself on my own. She got right to it, "Did you know my son, Mr. Conte?"

"No, I didn't."

"He was a wonderful person, always trying to help others."

"Yes, I have just begun to learn this.'

"I used to warn him all the time not to be so trusting, but that was his nature, he couldn't help himself." She paused for a moment. She was obviously hurting terribly. There was no pretense in this woman, I couldn't help but feel for her. "My husband tells me that you're the one whose going to find our son's killer."

My hands and feet had now also become cold, "I'm going to try, Mrs. Barnes."

Her eyes seemed like cameras, I felt like everything I did was being recorded. "Yes, Mr. Barnes has told me about the very generous reward he has offered you. I hope it's satisfactory?"

"Oh, yes, it's quite a bit of money."

"That's good. He also told you that we had our last detectives investigate you. I know this must be uncomfortable for you, but we felt we needed to know more about you. We wanted to make sure whomever we hired would have some feeling for a mother and father who lost their only son. We're convinced from the way you've struggled financially for your two daughters that you might have some idea what it's like for us." She paused for a moment, looking deeper into my eyes. "I'm now convinced that you are the one who will bring this fiend to justice."

My cold hands and feet meant nothing to my sweating forehead. "Mrs. Barnes, I'm not a superman. You must know I have no experience with homicide. But if the cops don't get the killer, I promise you, eventually I will."

She commanded, "Swear it."

I raised my hand up, "Eventually I'll get whoever it was, if the law doesn't do it first."

She then whispered to her husband who went off into the other room. Her eyes moved right back to me. "I know you will find out who did this awful thing. I must tell you something else." She paused once again. It looked as if a chill had run through her, "This murderous thing you are after, I feel its presence. Like it's here watching and listening to us. Sometimes I wake up in the middle of the night feeling as if it is somewhere in this house. I walk around, hoping to confront it, ready to destroy it."

Now she was beginning to get me a little frightened. Fortunately, Mr. Barnes returned before she could detect my uneasiness.

He carried with him three small boxes, which he handed to his wife. She opened each one individually. Upon inspection, a fleeting smile crossed her face. She then handed them all to me. "These are for your wife and two daughters."

I placed the boxes on my lap, opening up the one on top. Inside was a woman's gold watch set with diamonds. I was astonished, it was beyond attractive, it was exquisite and very expensive-looking. I shook my head no. "I can't except these. Thank you but this is impossible. You have already been more than generous. There's no need to give me anything else."

I held them out waiting for either one to except them back. But this was obviously all Mrs. Barnes' doing. She got up, saying, "No, young man. Except them for what they are. Consider them whatever you want—a bribe to even work harder—I don't care, just take them. Don't deprive your wife and daughters of this luxury. And remember, young man, be very careful. There is somebody very bad out there. Don't trust anyone." She got up, nodded, and left the room.

Mr. Barnes walked me to the door. I whispered to him, "I feel funny about this. I don't want to insult your wife and certainly I appreciate it, but it's way too much."

"Don't give it a second thought, son. It's just something my wife wanted to do."

We said our goodbyes. When I got back inside the Wagoneer, his words resonated in my head: "Don't give it a second thought." Yeah, sure. No problem. I'll forget all about it. . . .

I had thought a lot about Juju the previous night, wondering if he really was the killer? And if he was, could I turn him in? There wasn't much to think about now. The Barneses had me bought, totally. I not only wanted the one hundred thousand, I wanted to get the son-of-a-bitch who killed their son. Yet, Mrs. Barnes had painted the killer to be almost supernatural. On the contrary, Juju was anything but unearthly, except for his tremendous speed. . . .

I always got a kick out of driving to my house to see my kids; that is, it *was* my house until a judge awarded it to Sally. But it always frustrated me how close we had come to the neighboring

ED CALANDRO

Trumbull town line. It was a good neighborhood and all that, but it was still Bridgeport. That was the only reason we were able to afford the house.

I could see Jeanie and Sara waiting by the front picture window. They were my two sweethearts. Always loving and caring toward their dad, even during the hard times when their mother and I fought all the time. That wasn't the case any longer. The day after our divorce we started caring for each other again. I stuffed Mrs. Barnes' gifts into my jacket pockets and made my way to my three best girlfriends.

Sara was the first to greet me, "Daddy, Daddy!" She was up in my arms kissing me all over the face. I loved holding and kissing her, "Hi, puppy, how's my baby?"

She gave me a sweet look, planting a big kiss on my face, "Good, Dad. How's my Dadsy-foo?"

"I'm fine now, pup."

She slid down through my arms back to the floor. Standing behind her was Jeanie, wearing makeup. It wasn't kid's makeup, it was women's makeup. "Hi, Daddy."

"Hello, princess. You look beautiful."

She came over to kiss me. My nostrils flared as I caught the scent of her sweet perfume. After the kiss I asked, "What's all this? Are you looking to be grown up before your time?"

She looked hurt. "You don't like it, Daddy?"

"Oh no, baby, it's not that. It's just, aren't you still a little too young?"

Her mother answered before she could. "In four months she'll be thirteen, Jim. Besides she wanted to look pretty for you."

"She does look pretty for me and she always has."

My daughters, sensing the potential of an argument, each grabbed one of my hands—directing me over to the sofa. Soon after, with the aid of some 1991 rap music, I was treated to a

THE FOURTH ESTATE MURDERS

fashion show as Sally sat beside me telling me the cost of each garment and where they were bought while the girls showed them off. God, it was great to love and even greater to be loved.

The fashion show lasted a good hour. I didn't care. Prolonging dinner was okay with me, knowing it would be some type of soy bean product disguised as meat. Plus greens, all kinds of greens. Or if Sally wasn't in the mood to try and impress me, she'd serve what they ate mostly everyday, grains and beans. Whatever it was she served, it would usually take twelve hours or so for me to digest it.

After the fashion show, we talked about school and boyfriends. There was no need to worry about a roast burning because there wasn't one. As far as I was concerned that was the only good thing about grains. The more they cooked the easier they were to digest. I had thought about waiting until it was almost time to leave so I wouldn't have to explain where the jewelry came from, but the thought of further stalling the dinner was too irresistible to pass up. I announced, "I have a surprise for you all."

Sara began jumping up and down, but Jeanie remained reserved, asking, "Mommy, too?"

I gave her a look of appreciation, "Yes, Princess, Mommy too." I handed the less decorated watches to the girls and the other to Sally, presuming that's the way Mrs. Barnes wanted it. Screeches and squeals filled the room, along with plenty of kisses. The girls were beside themselves, and in no time were fighting for the phone. What was the sense of owning an expensive piece of jewelry if every person they knew didn't also know about it? Sally had said nothing but now that we were alone I knew that she wasn't just going to except the gift without an explanation. "What is going on, Jim? I called the mortgage company to see if you had paid them anything. They were very nice, saying you made five payments. Thank you. Then you give me five hundred dollars in cash; now this. I hope you are not doing something the girls will be ashamed of."

I understood her point, but she was always so darn righteous. Anytime she did anything to better herself, she automatically thought everyone else should do the same thing. She always judged people on how she thought they should be and not for what they were. There was no getting around it, she was a wonderful person, but if you gave her an inch she'd take that whole mile.

"Listen, Sally, contrary to your suspicious mind, I've never done anything my babies would be ashamed of. It's none of your business where the jewelry came from. If you don't want your watch, give it back and I'll pawn it or something, but the girls are keeping their watches."

That was it. She needed to say what she said, in order to be exempt from any wrong doing, and I needed to say what I said to let her know that she couldn't bully me. The watch was already on her wrist while her wet lips gently touched mine. The only thing this managed to do was wake up Hoppy who had been sleeping the past few days.

I put my arms around Sally, I wanted her more these days than I had ever wanted her before. I began rubbing my hand over one of her full breasts, with Hoppy sending messages to go for it. Using a mirthful voice she uttered, "Stop, Jimmy, please, the girls." Then she put her wet lips to my ear, whispering, "Come back later tonight."

I wanted to stick my hand up between her legs for a little inspiration to keep me going until I could get back, but the giggles from my two daughters who were looking on, caused their mother to playfully slap me. "Stop it, Jimmy."

Dinner wasn't so bad after all. My good brother-in-law Frankie

THE FOURTH ESTATE MURDERS

and my sister Mary had been over that afternoon bringing with them a sort of "care package" of homemade sauce. In it was a few pounds of organic spaghetti plus some fresh tomatoes and vegetables which made for a very pleasant dinner. Frankie and Mary, it was hard to find better people than them.

Our daughters dominated the evening, always encouraged by having the four of us together again. They'd never entirely given up hope that we could bring back what we once had. Deep down they must have truly known that there was no turning back for any of us.

When it came time to leave, the three of them begged me to stay longer, but I insisted I had work to do. Sally walked me out to the Wagoneer. "Do you really have to go, Jim?"

"Yup, I have some work that can't wait."

"Oh sure, on top of some young, blond bimbo, no doubt."

This was a really old argument, not entirely without validity.

"I thought I was invited back here tonight?"

She looked as though I had complimented her. "Well, if you really want to."

"Want to! I'd beg if you asked me to."

She leaned over and kissed my cheek, "Well, maybe I will." And off she hurried back into the house. . . .

Driving down Main Street heading toward the center of Bridgeport, it didn't take long for my thoughts to leave the sweetness of my family. I knew where I might be able to find Juju. If you were one of the "Old Guard" blacks in this city, you could usually be found at one time or another at Art's Cotton Club. I figured, sooner or later, I was going to have to go there. I might as well go now. It still wasn't real late in the evening so it wouldn't be that crowded.

Art's Cotton Club was in the center of the old time black

section on Railroad Avenue. Nowadays blacks were living in just about every neighborhood of Bridgeport. That wasn't bad. They were just like the rest of us, evasive and cold-shouldered to the new welfare arrivals who had poured into our city the past ten years. However, Art's still did a thriving business mostly because local black celebrities, such as Juju, still frequented the place. The only problem was, except for an occasional white woman, practically no other whites went in there; so it was unlike its famous Harlem big sister, The Cotton Club, which the whites literally poured into.

As soon as I walked through the door I realized the loud music was the same music my daughters had modeled their clothes to. It wasn't as bad as I had anticipated. I probably got less looks than one of the "brothers" would get in an all-white bar. Art's had a long narrow bar area that opened into a back room with a few pool tables, a dance floor and a small stage. Somewhere near the back end of the bar, I sat down. The bartender was on me like a bee on honey. "Hey, man, what's happinin'?"

"How are you doing? I'm looking for a friend."

He took a step backwards, "Ain't you in the wrong place?"

I couldn't help smiling. He was a good-looking guy, well built, light-toned face. "Naw, I'm not kidding. I'm looking for Juju Sims?"

"What are you, some kind of cop?"

He spoke a little too loud because a few other people heard what he had said. I made sure I spoke even louder, "No, man. I'm no cop. Juju and I grew up together."

A short man walked over to us, "Shoot, Bro, I knows y'all. You be James Conte. Shoot, Harvey, this here boy can hit the baseball further than y'all can fire a bullet from that .38 o' yours."

The bartender laughed, looking at me, "Who in hell is James

Conte?"

I returned his laugh, "Well he isn't any James Brown, that's for sure."

He laughed as he stuck out his hand. "I'm Harvey."

We shook hands, "Call me Jim."

"Hey, I call everybody "Jim". I'm going to call you Joe Dimaggio."

The old man interrupted, "Don't y'all mind Harvey, he don't think his shit smells like the rest o' ours."

"Get the hell out of here, you old black dog, before I bring out your bar tabs."

That's all it took, the old man gave me a pat on the back and left.

Harvey asked, "What do you want Juju for?"

I reached in my pocket, pulling out a twenty. I pushed it to him, saying, "It's private, I need to speak to him."

He looked at the twenty and then at me, "I'll tell you right now, Joe Dimaggio, this ain't the 1940's. A twenty dollar bill will buy you a couple of drinks, or maybe one of them whores down the other end of the bar will let you hold one of her tits for a few minutes."

I pushed the twenty closer to him, asking, "Can I at least buy a beer?"

"Shit, this'll buy you maybe ten beers, fifteen if you were a nigger."

He had already uncapped a Miller for me and was pouring it in a glass when he saw the hundred dollar bill laying on the bar. His face lit up. "Is that there dead president for me?"

I looked at Franklin's face on the bill, he was never a president I thought. "Yup, it's all yours."

He walked off to where a couple of fellows were shooting pool and whispered something to one of them, who immediately left.

ED CALANDRO

He returned to pick up the Ben Franklin, then went about his business.

I sat there by myself thinking about Juju. Back in the early Seventies, long after we'd both graduated from Central High, I met Juju at a swanky party in Westport, Connecticut. At that time my new friends were calling me James, but that was nothing to the young black I met there called Abdul. When Juju realized it was me he was being introduced to, he made like he had never met me before. I did the same. Neither one of us wanted to divulge that we were a couple of Bridgeport rats. I couldn't get over how good had Juju looked. But he had always been good with costumes. I guessed it was because he was always trying to get involved in dramatics. That night he was with his friends and I was with mine. Later in the evening we smoked some pot together. That was all it took, from then on everytime we looked at one another, we started laughing. I don't think I ever laughed as much as I did that night. It felt great to fool people.

Shortly thereafter, I met Sally, and a little while later became Jimmy again. I couldn't recall exactly when Abdul had changed back to Juju, but he had, or at least I thought he had.

I always thought Juju should have been a singer, his voice was so smooth. "Hey, Jimmy, what are you doing here?"

My legs shook. How was I going to do this? I turned to him, "Juju, it's been a long time. Harvey, give Juju a drink."

Right away I could tell he knew something was wrong. He sat down beside me. "What's up, man?"

"Oh, the same old shit. How about you? What are you doing these days?"

Harvey set a mixed drink in front of Juju. I asked the bartender, "How did you find him so fast?"

Juju answered, "I just pulled my car into the back parking lot. All he had to do was send someone out to get me."

Harvey beamed, "Well, man, I guess you are just like a nigger now. From now on you get fifteen beers for your twenty."

He walked off. Juju asked, "What's Harvey done? He cheat you? He cheats everyone."

I said nothing for a moment, thinking it would be impossible to play any games with him. "Listen, man. I've got to talk to you. Do you want to go inside my car where it's private?"

He scowled, "What the fuck do you want, Jimmy?"

I figured now was as good a time as any, I whispered, "Did you know a man by the name of Morgan Barnes?"

"What kind of shit is this, Jimmy?"

I thought that this could get nasty, not unlike the fight that Juju and I had gotten into when we were kids. I figured he might as well know right now. I looked him straight in the eyes and readied myself just in case he was going to throw a punch at me. "I've been hired to find the person who killed Morgan Barnes. I got some information yesterday that led me to you."

He was shaking his head. It was easy to see he was getting real angry. "So, you've stopped following cheating husbands? Now you've become a complete scumbag . . . you think I might be the killer, huh? What if I am? You gonna take me in, brave boy?"

"Did you kill him?"

"None of your fucking business."

"Somebody told me you iced him, Juju?"

"No shit, you white, mother-fucking trash. That greasy wop Louie Rosselli told you, right?"

Juju had gotten real loud. A number of people had gathered around us to listen in on what we were talking about. I was becoming increasingly frightened. At this point I figured—what the hell, I'd started it, I might as well follow it through. "Did you strangle him, Juju? Did you kill the poor guy for a broken-down building?"

His answer was first a left then a right fist to my face. I lunged at him and both of us went crashing to the floor with me landing on top. I tried to pin him so I could put at least one of my fists to his face. We struggled, neither one of us able to get off another punch. I felt that I needed desperately to hit him back. There was no way that he'd let me get my arms up high enough to launch one to his face, so I started punching his body. He began doing the same to me. We rolled around the floor hitting any part of each other's body we could. Somebody grabbed me around the neck, pulling me off Juju. Harvey stepped between us, looking my way while a few people held Juju back from me. Harvey yelled, "You're a trouble-makin', white, mother fucker. You get your ass out of here right now." He ordered the man holding me, "Let him go, Billy."

As soon as Billy let me go, I pushed Harvey out of the way and landed one solid on Juju's face while two men were still holding him.

Four or five people jumped on me and in the process I took a few more punches, but it was worth it. I could hear Juju screaming in the background. They dragged me to the door and actually threw me out.

I stumbled to the Wagoneer, got in, drove to the nearest phone booth and called Tommy. His wife, Alice, answered. I spoke to her as politely as I could, trying like hell not to swear. She hated curse words. Finally she stopped asking me questions about my daughters and let me talk to her husband.

Tommy sounded like he had been sleeping. "Hello, Jimmy, what's up?"

I had been getting myself all worked up, "Listen, Tommy, tomorrow morning the first thing you do at work is get one of your bigwig, corrupt, cop friends to get me a pistol permit. Got that?"

"Yeah, yeah. Where are you, Jimmy? Are you in some kind of trouble, or what? Tell me where you're at, I'll come and get you."

I paused to catch my breath. I had gotten Tommy good and riled. "I've got to go, I'll talk to you tomorrow."

"Wait, Jimmy, don't hang up!"

I hung up on him. I thought he might get a little bit frantic, maybe even curse a few times in front of Alice. That would be some consolation.

I drove down to Seaside Park. It used to be Bridgeport's beautiful beach on the Long Island Sound. Now it looked like a place too dangerous to walk at night. Garbage and debris blew along the sand and roadway. I parked the Wagoneer and walked down to the water. Squatting down, I brought some of the cool, salted sea to my face. Juju really got me good. I could only hope the one I nailed him with did some damage. I got back up and looked across the sound to Long Island and yelled as loud and as long as I could. . . .

I had only been back in the car for a few minutes when Hoppy reminded me where we were supposed to be. The old Wagoneer scooted through central Bridgeport, all the way up to North Main Street and almost out of Bridgeport, but not quite.

She had left the outside light on. It didn't matter, I was going in even if it wasn't. She greeted me at the door in her night clothes. Sally used to wear alluring nightgowns all the time. Now it was flannel pajamas and furry little rabbit slippers.

Once I got in and under the light she gave me a horrified look, whispering, "What happened, Jimmy? Oh, my God, you've been in some sort of fight."

I placed my hands on her waist, pulling her toward me. She

sounded concerned, "Let me get some ice. You might have a black eye tomorrow."

I put my lips on her neck, nibbling the coolness of her soft, luscious skin. She moaned softly as my tongue moved up to her ear while one of my hands was unbuttoning her flannel top. Once the hand was inside, it felt blessed while the other hand that held her wanted to touch her delicious breasts, also—as did my mouth. We were quietly making our way to the bedroom, all the time exploring the parts of one another we hadn't enjoyed for way too long. I could feel her body shudder a few times. I realized I'd have to restrain myself or she'd get out of control before we even made it to the bed. I moved one of my hands between her legs. That brought on another moan. She took the opportunity to go after Hoppy who was waiting, proudly. She couldn't move her hands fast enough to free him from his hideout. She began stroking it reverently and in no time we were on the bed. I was hardly given the chance to further touch her. Laying on my back with my legs off the end of the bed, she kissed Hoppy, continuing to stroke it while finishing the job of removing all my lower garments. Then she put Hoppy in one of its all-time favorite places—inside her mouth. The slurping sounds she was making sounded like an overture to a beautiful, erotic symphony we had begun.

Finally she moved her legs onto the bed. I seized the opportunity to immediately strip her of her pajama bottoms. To my delight, that's all their was. I placed my palm on her bush, her legs spread open, she was already soaked with juice. My fingers slipped easily in and out of her seeping crevice, probing for the turnkey that unlocked sexual stimulation. Once the clitoris was located, all hell broke loose. She squealed, then shivered, panting heavily. She moved her mouth away from Hoppy, leaving one hand on it to keep it satisfied, while she kissed her way up to my chest. I wanted to put my mouth on that delicious pussy of hers, but whenever she got like this she became very greedy to be fucked. I was helpless; she would take over. She had Hoppy in one hand and me exactly where she wanted me, flat on my back. She placed one leg over the top of me and eased her wet honey pot on down over Hoppy. She wanted to buck and ride, but she was still too tight. Now that she was where she wanted to be, we were both equally happy. We would make our sweet music for as long as we could last. Sex, at the very least, is always good, but when you do it with someone you love, it is heavenly.

SEVEN

It was the middle of the night before I got back to the office.
I fell into a sound sleep only to be awakened by that same
embarrassing dream. Far off there was a voice calling, "Jimmy,
wake up. C'mon, get up."

I opened my eyes. Standing before me was my jolly-looking
friend. "What time is it, Tom?"

"It's time for you to get the hell out of bed. You shit-head,
Alice and I spent the whole night awake worrying about you."

"For what?"

He started to yell, "For what? For what? You call up and tell
me you need a weapon immediately, then hang up on me!
Where're your fucking brains?"

I yawned, "Oh yeah, that's right. I forgot." I looked at him. He
wanted to stay mad at me, but there was no way he could. His
voice softened, "Who the hell put that little mouse under your
eye?"

I put my hand to my eye. "Ouch! Juju Sims."

"What!?"

"Yeah. I got into a fight with Juju last night."

He laughed, "I told you the other night, you're turning back
into Wild Man Conte again."

"Not hardly. I was questioning Juju on the Morgan Barnes
case."

Tommy sat down on the side of my bed. I told him the whole
story. The series of articles Morgan Barnes had been doing, how

THE FOURTH ESTATE MURDERS

I found out it was Louie Rosselli who owned the apartment house, and how Louie fingered Juju. And, of course, how Juju had taken offense to my inquiries.

Tommy's mouth gaped open, he asked, "Juju killed Morgan Barnes?"

"Naw, no way. Rosselli is full of shit."

"How do you know Juju didn't do it?"

"His fists told me. That's how."

"That's it?"

"Yes. I just don't think he'd get so insulted if he was the killer. Besides I should have known it wasn't him. This killer is somebody real nasty. Tommy, trust me, Juju didn't do it."

"Sure, but why do you say, nasty?"

"I saw Morgan's mother yesterday. She seems to feel the killer was someone real evil."

"No shit. Whoever it was strangled her son."

"You don't understand what I mean—like a psycho, a nut. I feel it too, Tommy. There's somebody real bad out there."

Tommy looked puzzled, "What are you going to do?"

"Start all over again. This time with a weapon of some kind. I don't know how I'm going to do it, but I have to talk to Juju again—and Louie Rosselli, too."

Tommy reached inside his jacket, pocket pulling out a small pistol. "Here, it's a Beretta, .25 caliber. I'll have you a license for it by the end of the day."

I looked at the tiny pistol and smirked, "What the hell am I supposed to do with that, go squirrel hunting?"

"What do you want, a big .357? You don't even know how to handle this thing, let alone a bigger pistol. Don't you remember what happened at the Police Academy? Besides, this will slow up any man at close range. I suggest if you're about to get into a fight with anyone that you run, if the opportunity arises. If not, shoot them with this—don't worry, it'll probably stop 'em."

I took the dinky Beretta and the box of shells. He was right, this would be all I'd need.

Tommy asked, "Where the hell did you end up last night?"

"I went over to see Sally and the girls."

"Oh-ho, starting it up again. I knew it."

"You don't know shit—absolutely nothing."

"Jimmy, she's the best thing that ever happened to you. Can't you see that?"

"I know, Tom, you're right. She's a beautiful person. We've just gone our separate ways. We've grown too far apart to ever compromise. If we could spend ninety percent of our time in the bedroom, things would be great."

He yelled, "You and that dick of yours! When the hell are you going to learn?"

"Learn what? There's nothing left to learn. What am I going to do? Go back home and eventually open a health food store with Sally? No, I'm going to continue working, and put my babies through college, then get the hell out of Bridgeport; and if I happen to get laid a few times along the way—well then, so what."

Tommy rubbed my head like I was a little kid. "Listen, Jimmy, I've got to go to work. I'll see what I can do about getting you more information today. I've got to tell you, I'm a little worried the police might find the killer before we do."

I shrugged my shoulders, "Tommy, I'm doing the best I can, I'm no Sam Spade you know."

He gave me a strange look, asking, "Are you absolutely sure Juju didn't kill Morgan Barnes."

"Positive."

"Are you going to be at the Stayawhile tonight after I get off work?"

THE FOURTH ESTATE MURDERS

"I'll try to be there."

I left my office, not even bothering to listen to my messages on the telephone answering machine. I was sure that most, if not all, the calls were from Tommy. Probably cursing me for not being there last night.

I walked down the street to the Main Line Diner to get myself some desperately needed coffee and breakfast.

Gerty, my waitress, was going to be the first of many to ask, "Who'd you upset so much?"

"I fell out of bed."

She sarcastically laughed, "Yeah sure, Jimmy, more like some irate husband kicked you out of his wife's bed."

"Just get me some coffee, will you?"

"Alright already; touchy this morning."

She brought over a coffee and the morning Telegram. I ordered eggs over easy, ham, some home fries and well-done rye toast. I was just about to open the paper to the sports section when I saw the front page headline: MURDER IN POST-TELE-GRAM PARKING LOT. The story was entitled: "The Post's James Walblont Brutally Slain." This was big news for Bridge-port. Enough so that it took the front page away from the popular war.

I knew who Walblont was. His column always irritated blue-collar people. He was so high and mighty. I guessed he'd gotten somebody very mad. Again I was about to turn to the sports section when I noticed another story on the killing with dark letters saying: "PRELIMINARY AUTOPSY SHOWS VAST QUANTITIES OF SNAKE VENOM INJECTED INTO THE DECEASED."

Gerty banged the plate on the table, my signal that it was time to eat. I read on, while devouring my breakfast. The details were sketchy, but very gruesome. This was obviously carefully premeditated, something an extremely depraved person would do. When I finished breakfast I got on the phone as quickly as I could. After a few rings the answer came, "Bridgeport Police."

"Tommy, it's Jim. Is anyone else listening in on this line?"

"I'm going to put you on hold, Jimmy." In thirty seconds he was back on, "What's going on?"

"Tom, I need everything you have on the James Walblont murder, pronto, tonight—got that?"

He whispered, "Got it. You be careful out there. Don't forget to load the Beretta."

I thought . . . Don't forget to load the Beretta! I forgot to bring the darn thing.

I figured I better start getting used to carrying the mini-pistol on my person, and I would; but first I wanted to pay a visit to the Post building.

The killing had occurred yesterday morning. I presumed Bridgeport's finest had already reenacted the murder scenario. Tommy would no doubt provide me with the information this evening. I was curious as to who would be the detectives on the case. And whoever they were I wondered if they had the same hunch as me. I thought if I was going to get anywhere on this case, I couldn't be worried what the cops were doing. I had to just go for it, while remaining as secretive as possible.

I drove through the parking lot and, sure enough, there were a few uniformed cops along with some plain-clothes detectives. I parked out on the street so none of them would recognize me. Once I entered the building, I scanned the directory hoping Walblont's name and floor number would be on it. No such luck. So I walked right into the main lobby. I had all kinds of I.D.'s, but when I saw who the receptionist was I realized none would be necessary.

THE FOURTH ESTATE MURDERS

She had her head down, seemingly looking through a roladex. I tried to make my voice sound low and sexy. With her as my inspiration, that would be no problem. "Hello, Linda."

She looked up, already a bright smile on her face. "Jimmy! Hello, baby. Where have you been?"

"Been busy, honey, but I was in the area. I figured you wouldn't mind if I feasted my eyes for a while."

She giggled, showing me a little more of herself. "How did you know I worked here?"

I tried a simple lie, "Oh, I called you a few times. One time somebody answered and told me you work here."

"You must mean Sheila."

"Yeah, Sheila . . . I've been wondering when we were going to go out again. Sometimes I wake up dreaming about you, Linda.'

She looked slightly confused, "Why dream when you can have the real thing?"

Hoppy started sending messages to forget about the investigation and grab Linda. "When can I see you?"

She pushed the blond hair away from her eyes. "Tonight, if you want."

"Oh, yes, I do. But it's going to have to be real late."

"What time?"

"Midnight."

She shrugged her shoulders, "I'll be waiting."

Jeez, I was getting ready to turn around and walk away, momentarily forgetting my mission. Fortunately her ambrosial smile kept me in a trance. "Anything exciting ever happen around here?"

She put her dumb blond look on. "Exciting! Well, one of our reporters was murdered yesterday. Don't you read the papers, honey?"

"Oh, no! Who did it?"

"They don't know for sure. But they think it's the Puerto Rican boy."

"What Puerto Rican boy?"

"Oh, he came in here a few days ago and asked to see Mr. Walblont." Her voice cracked a little. "And I'm the one who told him Mr. Walblont was on the fourth floor."

"Oh, dear, I'm sorry, sweetie. You must feel awful. Were you able to identify him for the police?"

"Yes, but they told me not to talk about it."

"Gosh, you're their only witness?"

She shook her head yes, and then no. "Well, there's me and Leslie Van Houten."

"Who the heck is she?"

Linda wiped her dainty nose with a tissue, "She's a reporter. She had the desk next to Mr. Walblont's."

I placed my hand on hers, "I'd better let you get back to work. Don't go blaming yourself, Linda, honey. I'll see you at around midnight, okay?"

Her soft fingers caressed my hand, "I'll be waiting."

I walked toward the front entrance, but instead of exiting, I made a quick right for the elevators.

The fourth floor represented the classic newsroom—an area the size of a small gymnasium, filled with desks back to back. I stopped a young man carrying a load of papers. "Can you direct me to Lesile Van Houten?"

He pointed with his head and nose, "That's her over there with the dark suit on."

Standing talking to a few gentlemen was an average-height, slightly-overweight lady somewhere in her middle thirties. I walked slowly toward her, not yet exactly sure what I was going to say. All three turned to me as I had come too close for them

THE FOURTH ESTATE MURDERS

not to notice. I tried to be as polite as possible. "Miss Van Houten?"

"Yes, can I help you?"

"Well, yes, but it's kind of private."

One of the men standing with her stepped forward. "Who are you?"

I put my hands out, "Please, I don't mean to alarm anyone. I can understand your concern considering the recent events."

I reached into my wallet, pulling out my card with the Mutual Trust Insurance Company name on it. I handed it to her. "I'm a licensed detective who often works for Mutual Trust. You can easily check that by calling the insurance company, including its president, Calvin Thornebuckle."

I wasn't really lying, and if they did call, Mutual Trust would probably verify that I did work for them. Hell, their president recommended me to the Barneses.

She handed the card to one of her associates and asked, "What do you want?"

She wasn't great looking, but she had an attractiveness. I stuck out my hand, "First of all let me introduce myself. My name is James Conte. And if it's at all possible I'd like to talk to you in private."

She nodded, "Okay. I'll see you later, fellas."

I followed her as she walked ahead of me speaking as she moved, "I suppose this concerns James?"

"I'm afraid so."

"As you must know, I've already told the police everything I could."

"Is it possible to repeat it again for me?"

She turned and stared at me. It looked as though she had the slightest hint of a smile on her face. "What's this all about?"

"It's an insurance matter. Maybe you should call up Mutual

Trust, it might motivate you to be a little more cooperative."

"Oh, a detective who wants to be a cop." She stuck both of her hands out in front of me, asking, "Do you want to handcuff me?"

I gave her my most friendly smile, "Don't tempt me."

She glanced at her watch, "You've got twelve minutes, then I'm off to lunch."

"Why don't we have lunch together. Mutual Trust would be happy to treat us."

Now she looked puzzled, still with that almost-smile on her face. "Are you really who you say you are?"

I shook my head because she still doubted me. "We are not going to enjoy this at all unless you talk to someone. Look, either call the insurance company or the Bridgeport Police. Ask to speak to Sergeant Harrington, he knows I'm on this case."

She did just that. Tommy must have laid it on heavy. After she hung up she said, "Alright, but if this is going to be a long business lunch, I want to go somewhere expensive."

I nodded, "Sure, no problem, but it doesn't have to be all business." Hoppy sent signals of approval. Now, all we had to do was get out of the building without Linda the Receptionist seeing us.

Once I got her inside the Wagoneer, I figured I'd take her to Frankie's in Milford. It was only ten minutes away. Driving there, I tried to make her feel as comfortable as possible. I had her for the whole lunch hour. There was no need to rush into an interrogation.

She seemed like a nice, game, friendly person. But her work for the Post was really weird—she wrote obituaries.

Lunch time had already started at Frankie's. When we pulled up, my companion said she had heard of the restaurant. As soon as we entered, Romeo, the bartender, yelled, "Jimmy, twice in one week. I'll tell Frankie you're here."

THE FOURTH ESTATE MURDERS

She pulled my shirt sleeve, "We know the owner. I'm impressed, Mr. Conte."

"He's my brother-in-law, and will you please call me Jimmy."

Before she could reply, Frankie came walking out. "Jimmy, what's going on. Mary still doesn't believe you showed up the other day. Now today again."

Frankie hugged me as usual, then I introduced them, "This is Miss Van Houten, or is it Mrs.?"

"It's Miss, and please call me Leslie, Frankie."

Frankie smiled, "I'm kind of busy right now, but I'll talk to you a little later. Where do you want to sit?"

"Someplace private, Frankie."

We were seated at a quiet corner table. Within five minutes fresh breads were brought out with some diced, cold tomatoes in olive oil with oregano and cheese on top. Also a jug of red house wine. She looked as excited as a school girl. "You asked Frankie to call you Leslie, does that include me also?"

Her slight smile broadened. I hated to do it, but now was as good a time as any. "Can you tell me about James Walblont?"

She offered a pleading look. "Do I have to? Can't you read the police report?"

"How about if I ask you a few questions that maybe the police didn't ask?"

"Go ahead."

"Did you like Mr. Walblont?"

"Not really, he wasn't a bad person, just a little too stuffy for me."

"What were his columns about?"

"Oh, he was liberal, that's for sure. But everyone in the newsroom said he always bent the truth to his way of thinking."

"Who was the young Latin you and the receptionist identified?"

"He was a messenger. He brought James a small package."

"What was in it?"

"I don't know."

"What happened to it?"

She shook her head, "I haven't any idea."

"Did the police search his desk?"

"Of course."

She allowed me to question her for a good fifteen minutes. Having described the young Latin as best she could, her own opinion was that he was a nice person and probably didn't have anything to do with the killing. She had been with the paper for only a year and a half, and Walblont's desk-neighbor for the past three months. I got a definite idea that most of Walblont's peers didn't think he was a responsible journalist.

I needed more information, but the red wine was like an aphrodisiac. What I had earlier thought was a little excess weight on Leslie now looked like a healthy, full body.

Frankie's was almost filled to capacity, but that didn't stop Romeo from dropping off two small plates of linguini carbonara for us. She looked at me, almost embarrassed. "When do they show us the menu?"

Another sip of wine. I gazed at Leslie in an extremely fond manner, "No menu here for the regulars. Frankie feeds his customers individually."

She had just tasted the linguini. "Oh, good—there goes my diet."

"Diet! For what?"

I reached across the table feeling her shoulder and arm. "Oh, no, you don't want to lose any of that. You should treasure your body. Thank God I came along when I did. You probably would have been eating cottage cheese this afternoon. I want you to enjoy every bit of this meal."

THE FOURTH ESTATE MURDERS

She sipped her wine. That slight smile of hers was growing.

Leslie was thirty-four years old. Before she came to the Post, she had been a commercial artist. During that period she lived with the same man for eleven years. A year and a half ago she walked out on him; they had not seen each other since. She had no steady companion in her life as she spent most of her time trying to advance her career as a journalist. She claimed that two men less qualified than she had advanced ahead of her, mainly because they were men. The obituaries, she assured me, were not her final stepping stone.

After our salad, we were served Mako shark steak, quick-broiled, basted lightly with olive oil and garlic. Shortly after we began enjoying this tasty tidbit, the sound of that oh-so-familiar voice made me look up, "Jimmy, what da hell ya doin' here again?"

I got up to shake his hand, "We're eating, Len, sit down and have a glass of wine with us."

"No, can't. I got some bod-dee at da bar I gotta talk to." He looked at Leslie, "Who's da veal cutlet?"

"Oh! Leslie Van Houten allow me to introduce you to my other brother-in-law, Lenny, known fondly by his Christian name, Crazy Lenny."

"Hey, how ya doin', sweetie?"

She forced a smile, "Hello, Mr. Crazy Lenny." She probably had no idea what kind of man she was being introduced to.

He glared at her, "No, no, ya got it wrong, it's just Crazy Lenny. Mr. means tame and I'm wild."

Then he turned to me. "Hey Jimmy, I like dis one, she got a little meat on her."

I peeked over to Leslie who was barely maintaining her smile. Lenny mock-gestured a left and a right like a boxer. "Ba-bing, ba-boom, I gotta go, Jimmy. See ya later."

As he walked off I asked, "Hey, Len, any chance of seeing our friend again?"

He turned to me, looking serious, "Dat might not be so easy again, Jimmy."

"He lied to me, Len. I just have to ask him a few more questions."

He continued walking away then turned and bellowed, "I'll see what I can do."

Not only did he obviously make Leslie uncomfortable, but also many of the other diners. Lenny liked to do that. His whole personality was based on breaking the rules.

She looked at me puzzled, "What zoo does he come from? Is he really your relative?"

"Sure, he's married to my little sister, Josephine."

She brought a piece of Mako to her mouth, but hesitated then uttered, "The poor lady."

Frankie came over for a moment, choosing to sit by me. He wasn't like the king of his restaurant, more like a ruling philosopher. He looked at Leslie sympathetically, "You met our brother-in-law, Lenny?"

She didn't seem to quite know how to respond. "Yes, I did."

Frankie eased her mind. "He's something, isn't he? I have customers that call first to make sure he isn't here before they come."

"Oh, my gosh, really?"

"Yes, but in all honesty, Leslie, more people like him than don't."

She became a little curious, "Have you ever asked him to behave a little more . . . human?"

Frankie laughed, "All the time. Lenny tells me—if they don't like it, let them go and eat someplace else."

That left her mouth gaping open.

THE FOURTH ESTATE MURDERS

Shortly thereafter, Leslie looked at her watch saying she'd be late if we didn't leave soon. In five minutes we were back inside the Wagoneer heading back to Bridgeport. I had to stop at the turnpike rest area. All the wine I had drunk now beckoned to come out. I also took the opportunity to freshen up and clear my head. When I returned to the car, Leslie was doing the same as I had done, touching herself up for her return to work. Now that Hoppy was relieved of all that wine pressure, things were different. There was the most pleasant fragrance of her perfume captured inside the Wagoneer. It was like being in a world of our own. She turned to me only to see me staring at her. "Is something wrong? Are you alright?"

"I'm fine, just admiring your attractiveness."

"Oh, goodness, I think Mr. Conte has had a little too much wine."

"Well, maybe, and you sound like you haven't had enough."

"No, no, I've had plenty. Don't you think you should start your car. I'm going to be late as it is."

"I'm sorry, you're right, excuse me."

She seemed to like that. "There is nothing to excuse you for. I had a wonderful lunch. Unfortunately I'll have to go on a diet for another month, but it was worth it."

I exited into Bridgeport. I thought, soon I'd lose her. I had no time to beat around the bush. "Leslie, is there any way at all that I could take a look inside James Walblont's desk?"

"Oh, you're back to being the detective again."

"Yes, well, we both have our jobs to do."

"I could get in trouble, you know?"

"I'm always in trouble, but I wouldn't want that for you."

She sounded sarcastic, "You are so considerate, I'm sure you wouldn't."

I drove her to the side entrance of the Post building just in case the police were still out front. I pulled over, hoping I could at least get her phone number so I could ask her more questions when I needed to. She said, "Well, thank you for an absolutely fantastic lunch. As for you taking a look inside James' desk, I usually stop by here between ten-thirty and eleven o'clock each evening to see if anybody important died so I can have sufficient time to write up an obit. It's the best time because practically no one is in the newsroom then. If you want to come by tonight I'll leave your name with the front door guard, he'll allow you to come up"

I responded, "I'll be here for sure."

Off she went without another word.

I returned to my office. The answering machine was blinking for my attention. I didn't want to deal with it just yet, so I shut it off and went into the other room to lie down on the bed.

The dream, I was having the same dream again. Different scenes but the same old dream.

I woke up to the loud ring of my telephone. On the other end was the distinct the voice of a black man telling me Juju Sims was in the city jail and he had used his one call to get in touch with me, only to get my answering machine. This man urged me to get down to the police station right away, Juju needed to talk to me. . . .

When I walked inside the station I was disappointed to see Tommy wasn't behind his desk as usual. Instead it was Jerry Callahan, one of Tommy's protégés. "Hey, Jerry, where's Tommy?"

"Awh, he's with the mayor. Won't be back 'til later."

"Oh, shit . . . I need to see a guy. I think he's locked up here. His name's Juju Sims."

He looked through his book, "Yeah, we got him. He was arrested on a murder charge."

"What!? Jeez, Jer, I need to talk to him. Can you help me out?"

"Yeah, sure. Jus' remember to tell Tommy it was me who did you the favor."

He handed me a pass with Juju's name on it. "You know where to go, Jimmy."

I walked up to the third floor where the lock-up was. After I was searched, a guard let me through the first set of bars, then a jailer opened the second set of doors. He directed me. "All the way down to the end, in the communal cell."

I had stopped off to buy a few packs of cigarettes, taking them out as I arrived at the last cell. He was sitting down near the rear of the cell. I yelled, "Hey, man, I came as soon as I got your message."

He was up and to me in seconds. "Did you have anything to do with this, Jimmy?"

I handed him the cigarettes through the bars. "No, Juju, honest, I swear. I know you didn't kill anyone."

I looked over his shoulder to see who was listening, they all were. Juju also turned around, yelling, "Get the fuck away from us." He swung his arm out toward them and everybody moved back. He looked at me, pleadingly, "It's that fuckin' wop friend of yours—Louie. He set me up, I know."

That was a strong possibility. He beseeched, "Jimmy, you got to help me. I didn't do anything to harm anybody. I'll tell you who killed Morgan Barnes. It was that nigger friend of Louie's, Robin Harris."

"Robin Harris? I never heard of him."

"Yeah, I don't know him too well either. I only met him a few times at Louie's building, but I know he was doing something with Morgan Barnes."

"How do you know?"

"Because I tried to put together a compromise for Barnes on things that needed to be done to that building, but he told me Harris had already begun to satisfy his demands. Barnes wasn't a bad dude, but he had to be one of the worst newspaper people you'd ever meet."

I was confused. "This guy Harris, he was definitely black?"

Juju smiled, "Yeah man, you know we commit crimes sometimes, too." He looked through the bars, examining my face. My eye had never really swelled up too much. Some of the redness had already disappeared. He joked, "I thought I hit you a lot harder than that little mark."

"You did, you son-of-a-bitch. Don't think I won't remember. I'll get you back."

"You already did."

He moved his mulatto face right up next to the bars. Above his right eyebrow was a shiner, a very satisfying shiner. I whispered, "You see, you high-yellows can camouflage your wounds better."

His expression changed, he looked worried. "Jimmy, can you get me out of here?"

Knowing what Tommy could do, I felt confident. "Who were the arresting officers?"

"Some dudes named Jennings and Ivan King."

"What!?"

"Yeah, you know, Ivan the Terrible."

My stomach knotted up. Juju placed his hand on mine. "Can you do anything for me, Jimmy?"

I reached inside my pocket with my free hand, pulling out about one hundred dollars. I slipped it into his, saying quietly, "I'll do what I can to get you out of here. Take this money and I'll ask Tommy if he can get you a clean cell for yourself. Listen, Juju, I know you didn't do it. If you can think of anything else about Robin Harris, please tell me."

THE FOURTH ESTATE MURDERS

He shook his head. "Just his big feet, man. The dude had big feet."

That was just about it. The rest of the description could have fit half the black populace. . . .

When I returned to my office I did check the answering machine. There were loads of calls. One, of course, from Juju and a few from Tommy, along with various others. But there was a strange message from Mr. Barnes, saying simply that Mrs. Barnes hoped I was being careful and they would see me tomorrow at three as we had planned. Because we had made no such arrangements, I was puzzled. Maybe he was still disoriented from the loss of his son. I guessed I'd know what they wanted soon enough.

I called up the Bridgeport Police Station and with the touch tone pressed in Tommy's line. "Bridgeport Police."

"Tommy, it's Jimmy."

"Hey, how are you doing?"

"Not so good. I was just at the station. I guess I missed you. They got Juju locked up. Do you know anything about that?"

"This isn't a good time to talk about it, I'll see you in a little while."

"Yeah, I know. Look, before you get off I need to know if the New Haven Police have any idea of the weight of Barnes' killer from those footprints."

There was a moments pause. "It's a bad time, Jimmy. I'll see what I can do. Got to go. See you in about an hour."

I got cleaned up. While doing so, I couldn't get Mr. Barnes' message out of my head. He had seemed lucid in our previous meetings. Why now did he seem so confused?

It was blue-collar hour in the Stayawhile. All the working people were just coming in off their jobs—that is, those that had jobs. The place was full. As usual the cable station, CNN, was on reporting the latest results of that stupid war. I walked by Scotty, whose mailbag hung down next to his barstool. "Hey, Laddie. What did the Saudi say to the Iraqi?"

"What Scotty?"

"I said Bud Light not Scud fight."

I walked into the kitchen where Georgie was frantically cutting up salami on the meat slicer. It was times like these when he just couldn't do it all, that he'd break down. "Hey, Georgie, when are you going to hire someone to help out?"

He looked at me in a rage, "I no want anybody. I hate people. I maybe just going to lock these fucking doors one day. I jump off bridge, go ker-plunk, no more Georgie. Then see where these bastards go."

"Do you want me to pour some beers for you?"

"Oh, Jimmy, God-fucking-bless you."

Everyone was relieved. It wasn't like I had to mix any drinks, just pour beer or open bottles. I worked my way down the bar, filling each glass, or exchanging the empty bottles for full ones. I even knew what brands some of the customers drank. I came to an empty glass being used by a biker. I grabbed it asking, "What's in here, fella?"

"Ballintine Ale, man."

When I returned with the full glass of ale, he said, "Thanks, man, I hope ye ain't gonna chase me out like ye did my buddies."

He was another one of those middle-aged bikers—beard, long hair, chains. "No, that was a mistake. It's just that your motorcycles wake me up with all the revving they do. But I shouldn't have acted the way I did. I apologize."

"Shit man, ye ain't gotta be sorry. They were pussies, ye know what I mean? How 'bout yourself, can I but ye a beer, man?"

THE FOURTH ESTATE MURDERS

"Sure, thanks."

He stuck out his hand, "My name's Harland. How 'bout you?"

"Jim, Jimmy Conte."

I finished filling up the beer glasses and came out from behind the bar to drink my beer with Harland. He swiveled around on his barstool, we clinked our glasses together. "I have to ask you something, Harland. What do bikers do for a living?"

His icy look turned to a smile, showing off a gold tooth. "Shit, man, don't ye know? We're angels from Hell. There's plenty of ways to make money besides a steady job . . . what do you do, man?"

"I'm an investigator. I do work for private businesses or individuals."

"Ye any good?"

"I guess I'm alright. I've been doing it for a long time."

"What do ye investigate? Like, what are ye doing now?"

"Jesus, Harland, I can't tell you that."

"Hey, man, ye shouldn't use the Lord's name in vain."

What an odd dude. Deep down I had always thought bikers were like pirates. This guy confirmed it. He was a storybook biker. I glanced up at the television. He asked, "Are ye into any of this here shit?"

I shook my head. "Not really. I pretty much stick with sports. I'm for the Americans and all that, I just don't see the Iraqis having a chance. It's only a matter of time."

He pointed up to the screen, "How 'bout this shithead. Ye know him?"

I saw a familiar face on the tube. The noise was so loud I couldn't understand what he was saying. "Who is he?"

Harland swigged on his ale. "I'll tell ye who the motherfucker is, he's a fuckin' Commie. He's a son-of-a-bitch, bastard Commie."

Jeez, Harland, like I said, I pretty much stick to sports. Who is he anyway?"

"Shit, man, that's Peter Arnett. Where the fuck ye been? The scumbag's on the screen just about every hour."

We would have no doubt continued our delightful conversation if Tommy hadn't walked through the door. Harland swiveled back around on his barstool like most bikers would do when they see a uniformed cop approaching.

Tommy could be a real tough guy when he wanted to be. "What's wrong? Another asswipe biker come in the wrong door?"

I put my hand on Tommy's shoulder. "No, Tom. Come on, let's sit down—he's alright."

We began to walk away as Harland turned toward us. That's all Tommy had to see. He yelled, "You want something, dirt bag? You got a problem?"

I grabbed Tommy's arm just in case he decided to go for Harland, but the biker said nothing—instead turning back around to finish his ale, then leaving soon after.

I pushed Tommy into the booth. Georgie, who had caught up on his work, came over with a few beers. "Hey, Tommy, if you want, we take one of these shithead bikers out back and beat dog shit out of him."

That's what I liked about Georgie, he was so kind to his customers. I said quietly, "Georgie, why don't you shut up."

Tommy added, "All you have to do is sit by any one of those bikers and they'll all leave."

Georgie asked, "Why that?"

Tommy laughed, "Because you smell like a dead goat."

We both laughed at poor Georgie. "Yeah, two real funny guys. Next time me make either one you sandwich, I wipe my big balls on it first. Ha, ha, ha."

We both were duly repulsed, then Tommy asked, "What the

THE FOURTH ESTATE MURDERS

hell were you doing talking with that biker. I thought you might be looking for a fight again."

"No, he was alright. We were just having a conversation."

He didn't even seem to be paying attention. He got right down to business. "I've got some information for you."

Just then I realized he was using an evasive tactic on me. "Tom, the information can wait, I want to know about Juju."

He barked back, "What about him?"

"You know, Tommy, Ivan arrested him. Don't try and tell me you didn't have anything to do with that."

"So what if I did, nothing is going to come of it anyway. The New Haven Police haven't even come down to question him. What's the big deal?"

"No big deal, huh? You heartless rat. You and Juju grew up together. How could you do it to him?"

"Christ, Jimmy, we're talking about one hundred thousand dollars here. If anyone is going to find Morgan Barnes' killer it should be us."

I shook my head, "Oh, yeah. How about if the murderer has killed again?"

"Huh! Who?"

"Did you bring me anything on the James Walblont murder?"

Tommy's expression changed drastically. "Holy Mother of God. You think it's the same person who killed them both?"

"Could be, Tommy. I want to get this Juju thing out of the way first before we go talking about somebody killing newspaper people."

"What!?"

"Look, Tom, it's not going to put any money in our pockets having Juju behind bars."

"There's nothing I can do now. Juju is going to have to go through due process. Don't worry, Ivan's got nothing on him, he'll be out before you know it."

"Before I know it, huh? Tommy, what's happened to you?"

"Cool out, will you. If you feel so bad about Juju, give him part of your reward money when we collect."

I agreed. "Yeah, part of both our reward money."

"Oh yeah, and while we're at it. Why don't we give some to the freakin' United Negro Fund?"

I spoke as clear as I could, "Don't, I repeat don't let anything happen to Juju. I couldn't stand that."

"Christ, Jimmy, I didn't know you felt this way about Juju."

"You don't understand. I have my kids, you have your wife and kids. Other than that, the only thing we have is our past. It's me and you, Tommy, and every time I think of our past I can't help but see Juju there. He was better than you and me."

Tommy dropped his head, saying, "You're right, Jimmy, I shouldn't have done it. Even so, Jimmy, Juju may have been a better athlete than you, but he wasn't better than me."

Tommy and I could have spent the whole night arguing who was better, even in view of the possibility that we had a serial killer on our hands. I did like disagreeing with him, but so I chose to direct our conversation to the murders. "Listen, Tom, I think there may be a couple of ethnic groups that have been offended by some journalists, and killed them. Either that or there is somebody out there really good with disguises."

"You got any leads?"

"Not much. I'm thinking maybe we should hand it over to the police."

Tommy disagreed, "You're out of your mind. They don't know anything about this. If anyone can find out who killed these two guys, it's you, Jimmy."

"Yeah, great, but what if there is another murder? Do you want that on your conscience?"

"Christ, Jimmy, don't go talking like that. The only thing I have on my conscience is bills. You got that? Lots of bills."

Tommy was right. Most of the time that's all I had on my mind, also. We worked to pay our bills. He didn't take police graft, and I hadn't done anything to advance my financial position. We were staring at each other. I asked, "Alright, what do you have for me?"

Tommy pushed over a freshly photocopied file on James Walblont. "Jimmy, do you really think there's a plot to kill newspaper people?"

"Yes, I do. Neither one of the deceased had what it took. I think they're being killed because they are bad writers or something like that."

"Holy shit! You better watch yourself! Here's a temporary pistol permit for the Beretta. Where do you carry it?"

"Ah, I forgot it. I'll load it up before I go out tonight, I promise."

"You better. Where the hell are you going tonight?"

"First I'm going to the Post building. I met the columnist who had the desk next to Walblont's. I want to take a look inside his desk. Then I have a date."

He smirked, "I'll bet that columnist is a woman."

"Yup, you got it. Now how about the New Haven Police? Do they have any idea how much weight those footprints were carrying?"

He shook his head, "They never even bothered to try and figure it out."

We got up to leave. Every time I thought of Tommy going home, I thought of five, chirping, greedy, little birds in a nest all waiting to take everything Tommy had gathered.

I went up to my office to read the police report on the Walblont murder. Not much, other then they found a cowboy hat on the head of the deceased, plus one witness had claimed to have seen a man dressed in western clothes running behind the Post building. Either there was a bunch of lunatics or maybe one really clever one.

EIGHT

Paul Nelson stood inside his camper divesting himself of the latest disguise. After he had washed, he looked in the mirror at his naked form. He had, for some time now, thought of himself as an unpainted oil canvas. The body could be made up to look like almost anything. He had realized long ago that most personality types take their cues from one another—like scholarly people look like other scholarly people, construction workers look like other construction workers. In each separate group there are a few who look different—they try to look different. But the norm of each ilk mostly share the same characteristics. The deception of "disguise" is a simple matter of creating a persona that typifies a group as a whole rather than one of its odd-looking individuals. As for clues to detection, like fingerprints or hair samples, they were a simple matter—always protect your finger tips and either wear a wig of synthetic hair or leave behind strands of someone else's hair.

The image he saw in the mirror was becoming almost ghostly. He was beginning to think that he was flirting with invisibility. He reached for his tone-coloring makeup, applying the first shades of the character called Paul Nelson.

Ten minutes later, Paul Nelson put on a robe and sat down with the most recent newspaper. Scanning the pages he, recalled:

'SSportsss wheress ssportsss? Jimmy ssaid, I pretty much ssstick to ssportsss.'

He read article after article, ripping off the pages after he read them.

'Don't worry, my new friend. I will find a ssportsss writer for you. . . .'

The front door at the Post building was locked. I tapped on the glass and a guard, who looked like he had been sleeping, asked through the intercom, "Can I help you?"

"Yes, my name is James Conte. Miss Van Houten is expecting me."

He came to the door and let me in. "She's on the fourth floor, do you want me to show you the way?"

"No, that won't be necessary. I know how to get there."

He retreated to the desk where my date, Linda the Receptionist, sat during the day. He seemed to have gone soundly back to sleep even before my elevator door opened.

The fourth floor now was not the bustling place it had been this morning when I'd first come here. There were only a few people on the entire floor, one of whom was Leslie. She noticed me at just about the same time I saw her. We took our shortest routes through the desk aisles to greet one another. That slight smile was still there, showing off her sparkling blue-green eyes. She sounded almost impish, "I was wondering if you were going to show up."

"Are you kidding, this is the highlight of my week."

"Oh, yes, I'm sure."

We politely shook hands while she said softly, "Come on, I'll take you to James' desk, they haven't cleaned it out yet. Just make like we're good friends, okay?"

"That won't be hard. How about sweethearts?"

She giggled as she led the way, "You must still be feeling that wine.'

THE FOURTH ESTATE MURDERS

I laughed, "Yes, you're right, that must be it."

When we came to the desk area she and Walblont had shared, she sat on the top of hers, saying, "That's James', but don't touch anything—not right away, okay?"

I looked around the newsroom. There were a few people far away from us, but I understood her prudence. I sat on Walblont's desk and asked, "Anybody important die tonight?"

"No, just a few old ladies, but I'm sure they were important to their families."

"Are you going to write them important obituaries?"

"I already have, do you want to read them?"

Leslie showed me her work, which was neat and short. She looked around, scrutinizing the situation, finally saying, "Go ahead, have your look. I'll be back shortly."

I moved quickly and sat down behind Walblont's desk. The first drawer had typewriter paraphernalia. The second—personal stuff, photographs, awards, things like that. The third and largest drawer had books—a thesaurus and dictionary plus foreign language to English books. The top drawer was pens, pencils, erasers, all that type of material. Nothing really significant. I looked under the phone, through the telephone book, under the ink blotter—for a moment, nothing—then a folded piece of paper fell onto the hardwood desk from the bottom of the blotter. I unfolded it, not expecting to find what I did. It read:

I've read so much of what you've written
That it set my mind afire.
I read too much of what you've written
Telling me you stand for the liar.

Arnett was in the north while our boys died.
Dancing with the enemy while the mothers cried.

ED CALANDRO

*You have until tomorrow to unsay what's been said
or join the other that I made dead.*

I quickly stuffed it into my back pocket. My nerves were on edge for sure because drops of perspiration were landing on Walblont's blotter. A few moments later, Leslie returned. "Everything okay, Jim?"

"Ah . . . huh . . . yeah, I guess. Why?"

She looked at me as a teacher might a student. "Your face. You are sweating. Do you feel alright?"

"Yes, sure, I'm fine, I just get funny when I search through other people's stuff."

"Golly, a private detective with a heart. That's almost as bad as a journalist with a soul."

My mind whirled. I needed to concentrate on Leslie. She helped by walking over to me and dabbing my face with a tissue. It cooled me off some and allowed me an extra moment to think more clearly. I asked, "Does this mean you're a journalist with a soul?"

That smile, those sparkling eyes. Her attractiveness was forever growing. "Well you know, I've been here for a year and a half and I'm still writing obituaries. What do you think?"

I got up and out from behind Walblont's desk. "I think somebody around here doesn't realize what they have in Miss Leslie Van Houten."

She looked surprised. "You're finished already?"

"Yes, I am. If there were any clues, the police no doubt found them before me."

I was still shaky, knowing now that I was getting way out of my league. It seemed as though the robbing of the victim's belongings was just a deception. I had joked about it earlier, but now I was almost convinced it was one solitary person perpetrating all these dirty deeds. I needed to go back to my office. There was something in the Morgan Barnes file worth comparing with the Walblont file.

She seemed to be patiently waiting for me to return from my cogitation. I responded to her concern. "Oh, sorry. I need to go back to my office. Are you finished with your obituaries?"

"Yes, I am. Just waiting for you to finish."

She was too attractive to just say good-bye to. "Any chance of you coming with me?"

She had been wary of me right from the start. For whatever reasons, she remained so. "I can't do that. Why would you want me to?"

"For companionship. I feel a closeness to you."

She laughed, "That's what I'm afraid of. You remind me of one of those men who get into something just to get laid. I'm not looking for that."

I put my arms in a "hands off" gesture. "No romance, no touching, just conversation. Okay?"

She dropped her defense slightly, "What am I supposed to do, just throw caution to the wind?"

"Fling it out the window."

We took the Wagoneer, leaving her car in the newspaper's parking lot. On the ride over she did most of the talking. I learned that, in many ways, she and I were alike. Two estranged individuals in one of earth's most unbecoming dimples—Bridgeport. She had no one, having walked out on her lover after eleven years. She had done very well as a commercial artist, but claimed it was too lonely an existence for a single woman. So she switched occupations in mid-life, pursuing her college major—journalism.

We walked up the back steps so no one from the Stayawhile would notice us. I didn't know if she, or any woman for that matter, was ready for that unsavory bunch. When we entered my office she looked a little disappointed. "I was expecting a reception room with a desk and a dumb, blond secretary sitting behind it and your name—James Conte, Private Detective—etched on your door window. Something like Philip Marlowe."

"Oh, gee, I'm sorry to disappoint you. That's what I expected when I started out, too."

She shook her head in mock disappointment, "Tsk, tsk, I'm afraid there are no Humphey Bogarts left."

She seemed to be enjoying herself at my expense. I figured I'd sarcastically help her along. I opened the side door and flipped on the light switch, showing off the untidy room within. "I also live here; poor Bogey must be flipping in his grave."

"Yuk, I'm going to report you to the Society for the Protection of Debonair Nineteen-Forties Private Detectives. They are going to make you wear pinstripe suits for a year, Mr. James Conte."

She was becoming more comfortable around me. I liked that. Nonetheless, I still had detective business on my mind. I grabbed the Morgan Barnes file off my desk, excused myself and shut the bedroom door behind me. I hurriedly skimmed through the pages until I found it. The note the killer had left on the body of the victim. It was on police photocopy paper. I took the one I'd found under Walblont's blotter from my pocket. The words were pasted and printed on a glossy piece of paper. I turned it around. The message had been placed on an advertising flyer, offering a simple promotion: 'This spring at the Stratfield Theatre in Stratford Connecticut, King Lear, Richard the Third and Othello. Ticket information at all Ticketrons and the Stratfield Theatre box office'. There was nothing else, except for a small sketch of William Shakespeare in the middle of the flyer.

I vaguely remembered something about this from the other day, but I couldn't put my finger on what it was. It would almost

THE FOURTH ESTATE MURDERS

come, than I'd lose it. I looked at my wristwatch, it was close to midnight. I picked up the phone from my bedside table and brought it inside the closet with me. I quickly dialed Linda the receptionist's number, then shut the closet door. "Hi, Linda, baby."

"Hello, Jimmy, where are you?"

"I'm still working, honey. I was hoping to be finished sooner, but I still have more work to do."

Her voice was soft and sexy, she must have been dosing. "Oh darn, I bought such a nice outfit for tonight, Jimminy Cricket."

Hoppy started to rustle up, "Jeez, baby, don't say that, you'll make me feel guilty."

"Phooey on you. How about me? What time do you think you'll be finished with your work?"

My heart started pounding, "Oh, two, maybe three hours. Why?"

"Well, my roommate is away for the evening. I guess if you still want to, you can come over then."

"Baby, there's nothing else I want but to come over there."

What a voice she had, "Okay, Jimmy, I'm going to take a little nappy-poo, I'll be waiting."

I burst out of the closet putting the phone back by the bedside. Hoppy was so hard you could hang a wet raincoat on it. First I tried fanning it, then tapping it a few times. I sat down on the bed, panting. I tried thinking of anything to get my mind off Linda . . . the great catch Willy Mays made off Vis Wertz in the 1954 World Series. I'd seen the tape of that catch so many times. What happened to me? I should have been a baseball player. . .

I returned to my office, dropping the Barnes file back onto my desk. "Sorry I took so long, I'm sure Bogey wouldn't have kept you waiting."

"No, you weren't that long at all. Who are these two little

darlings you have hanging all over your wall?"

My favorite subject. "Those are my two babies. My sweethearts, Jeanie and Sara."

"Your daughters?"

"That's right."

"Where is your wife?"

I pulled out a photograph of her I had inside my desk. "This is Sally."

"No, I mean is she alive?"

"Of course! The girls live with her, we're divorced."

I was quick to quell her curiosity, grabbing her by the hand, "Come on, we're going to New Haven."

She offered no resistance.

The ride was great. She was treating me like a friend. Telling me all kinds of stories about her childhood. She sounded like she was a real happy kid. It was good to hear. These days most people told you about their unhappy childhoods and why they had so many hang-ups. Not her. Leslie was a slightly-overweight package of joy.

I made the exit into New Haven with her hardly even noticing. She couldn't stop talking. But then I turned down by New Haven Harbor. We drove down the deserted road; there was absolutely no one around. I glanced at her as we drove under a streetlight; there was some concern on her face. I tried to make her feel at ease, "I love it out here in the still of the night. I was down here recently during the day, it's just not the same."

She asked inquisitively, "What are we doing down here at this time of night?"

"Leslie, I'm disappointed, I thought you were beginning to trust me. The reason I was here the other day is that I was investigating an accident for an insurance company. When I filled out the report I forgot to put down the number on the telephone

THE FOURTH ESTATE MURDERS

pole closest to the accident.

I pulled the Wagoneer to the curb, stopping the car. I opened the door before she could reply. I said, "I'll be right back."

This was the spot. I looked around, the lighthouse out in the harbor blinked every four or five seconds—emitting a deep, foghorn sound. I swung around, looking at the skyline of the city, then the Connecticut Turnpike below it. In between were the two billboards, the first saying: 'Cranston Chocolates, how sweet it is'. And the second: 'This spring at the Stratfield Theatre. King Lear, Richard the Third and Othello. Information available at all Ticketrons.'

My God! The note, and this Shakespeare stuff. The killer was leaving clues.

Not wanting to worry Leslie, I hurried back to the Wagoneer. I pulled away without saying anything. She asked, "Well, what was it?"

"Huh?"

"What was the telephone pole number?"

"Oh! Oh, yeah, number fifteen."

At the beginning of the ride back to Bridgeport, I was pretty quiet. She asked, "Are you alright, Jim?"

"Yes, I'm sorry, Leslie. Sometimes I can't get my work out of my head."

I guess she figured I needed to think, so she turned the radio on softly to occupy herself. I immediately shut it off. "Why don't you tell me some more stories about when you were a kid?"

Her voice jumped up a few octaves. "Really? I wasn't boring you?"

"No, not at all. I loved them."

So, she started again, almost singing out the words. I listened for a few minutes, then switched my thoughts to the killer. I was almost sure it was a male, disguising himself as a young Puerto

Rican, a cowboy and probably a black man with big feet. I would definitely have to talk to Louie Rosselli again.

When I thought about the note I had found in Walblont's desk, I soon realized the killer had wanted the note to be read. He had wanted the police to know he was killing specifically newspaper people. It must have been only a freak accident that Walblont had stuck the note under the blotter and the police had failed to find it. Chills ran through me. This person was going to kill again, probably another newspaper reporter. I glanced over at Leslie, joyfully telling her story. That's what *she* was, a newspaper reporter.

Tommy seemed to have no confidence in his own police. I was beginning to agree with his assumption. Even if I did tell them my theories about the killer, they'd need something more concrete—if for no other reason then they were obliged by law to show physical evidence. I had no such obligations, there was nobody tying my hands. If ever I was sure of something, it was my theory about this killer.

We took the exit back into Bridgeport, with Leslie still narrating portions of her childhood. She interrupted herself. "Oh dear! Bah, blah—blah, blah, blah. I do go on, don't I?"

I had picked up snatches of her conversation, even though I'd fail if tested on it. But I had the gist of it. "I'd love to see some of your drawings and sketches someday."

"Really? You would? I'd like that."

"Well, when?"

"How about tomorrow night; dinner at my place?"

"A home-cooked meal, God, I'd love that."

"I don't know about home-cooked, I was thinking about sending out for Chinese."

"Well, then, a Chinese meal. I'd love that."

That look of distrust was on her face again. She quickly jotted

THE FOURTH ESTATE MURDERS

the directions down before I turned into the Post's parking lot. She pointed to her car. When I stopped next to it she waited for a moment then said, "That's it? No—'I'm feeling lonely tonight'? No—'Your perfume has made me dizzy'? This can't be it!"

I smiled confidently at her, "This is it, Leslie. Are you beginning to think you might have misjudged me?"

She stared into my eyes, then placed her soft hand on my cheek, saying, "No, I'm sure I haven't. But I'm really impressed, and I kind of like you, Jimmy Conte."

She opened her door before I could try to kiss her. "Tomorrow at seven, don't be late."

I waited until she was safely inside her car and had started it up. She seemed to recognize this gesture and gave me an "okay" wave. I took that as my cue to leave, and leave I did.

Late at night in Bridgeport I would usually run a red light or two. On this night, I ran them all. Waiting for me was the luscious, blond, Linda. Even though Leslie had charmed me silly most the evening, and I was on the trail of a nasty killer, I still had lustful thoughts of lovely Linda and what kind of scanty outfit she would be wearing.

NINE

There are all kinds of women in this world: Oriental, Hispanic, black and white; some Arabic ladies even cover themselves up, hiding their identity. All these women were making incredible advances within our society—becoming astronauts, doctors, pilots, and entering the business world—and still they all remain attractive females. I could only hope in this new, more perceptive feminine order there would always be a place for dumb, shapely, blonds like Linda the Receptionist.

I didn't leave Linda's apartment until after sunrise. When I returned to my office the first thing I noticed was the blinking answering machine beckoning for my attention. I felt guilty about not going over to it, relieving it of its burden, but I knew I should be in the shower clearing my head and preparing myself for what lay ahead. I was ready to stalk this diabolical killer, but I chose instead the comfort of my soft bed and soon after was in a deep sleep. The dream, the stupid dream. It was so easy to dream this dream. I wished I wouldn't have it anymore, but when it came—I welcomed it.

It was close to noon before I woke up. After my shower and shave, I sat down behind my desk and looked through all the information Tommy had provided on the murders. Where did I go from here? Sooner or later I knew I'd need to see Louie Rosselli again. This Shakespeare thing, was it coincidence? Did the killer want to be caught? Maybe it was a trap. I brewed a pot of coffee, hoping it would help to wake me up.

THE FOURTH ESTATE MURDERS

Indeed, the coffee had an effect. There's a fine line with coffee—when to drink it and when to stop. I poured a second cup and walked over to the answering machine. The first two calls were business related, I wrote down the names so I could refer them to a detective in Fairfield. We had ourselves a little reciprocal deal with our clients. For the next call there was only silence, a lot of people didn't like to talk to machines, then came a clear, terrifying message:

> *Beware, Fourth Estate, of what I say:*
> *No more journalistic lies, I pray,*
> *Taking liberties whenever you may,*
> *We now have Jimmy to witness the fray!*

I found myself in the bedroom getting the Beretta that Tommy had given me. I walked around the office with it, looking out the window to see if there were any suspicious people on the street; then under the bed, in the closet, in the shower. For a while I was frightened, almost panicky. Why not? It was the killer who called! He knew I was on the case, he even knew my name. Who wouldn't be concerned?

I played the tape over and over again. Almost every time I played it, I got a different kind of feeling. I listened carefully to every word. Now I was almost certain that it was only one person doing the killing. But there were two other things the message made quite clear. One was that he wasn't finished killing members of the press, and the other was that he called me a witness—like he almost welcomed my participation in this awful game he was playing.

I never should have accepted the case, now I was in way too deep. It reminded me of when I was a kid playing baseball. I could hit almost any pitch, but the good pitchers were harder.

There was one kid, Richie Bartek, he was the best. When I knew I was going to face him, I'd stay up most the night thinking of nothing else but him. Eventually we'd play the game and sooner or later I'd connect and get him. I had to believe I'd get this killer, too. Maybe he was the best at what he did.

It was a strange afternoon. I sat behind my desk for most of it. And at some point during the afternoon I came to the crushing realization that at thirty-nine years old I'd never make it into the Major Leagues. How very sad. It was the murderer who finally made me see that it was all over for me. If anyone could have seen me or known how I felt, they would have thought me so childish. Tears rolled down my cheeks. It was terrible to comprehend that I had peaked at what I did best at the tender age of sixteen. Everything after that was a slow ride downhill to where I was now. All of a sudden my confidence wasn't what it had been only hours earlier. It was this killer who was really good, not me.

Wallowing in my low spirits, I guided the Wagoneer to St. Mary's by the Sea. I was a little late for my appointment with the Barnses. I had no idea what they wanted, nor was I prepared to report on my progress as I had on my last visit. I tried desperately to bring myself into an upbeat mood. It gave me some inner amusement to think that the only thing that worked were thoughts of Linda the Receptionist.

Mr. Barnes opened the door before I even had a chance to knock. He put his finger to his lips signaling for me to say nothing. I nodded and followed him inside. Mrs. Barnes was sitting in the large parlor. She, too, offered no words, instead showing an emotionless face. I continued following Mr. Barnes over to a painting. He took it off the wall showing me the reverse side. What I saw was definitely a wireless bug. I took the painting from his hand and easily disconnected the microphone, saying, "I'm going outside to take a look around."

Out by the street on an inside portion of the stone wall, hidden from the house by an evergreen, was the tape recorder/receiver.

I brought it back inside, placing it on the coffee table in front of the Barneses, "I think this should be it. The son-of-a-gun has been listening to your conversations."

Mr. Barnes looked confused. "But why?"

"I don't know. Maybe the bug has been here a while. Maybe your son brought the killer to your home while you were away. Maybe he wanted to keep tabs on you, learning how dedicated you are to finding him."

Mrs. Barnes interrupted, "Why do you refer to the murderer as 'he'"?

I hated this, having to talk to her while she showed so much pain. "He called me yesterday, leaving a message on my answering machine."

She stared deep into my eyes. "Then you are close to him?"

"Yes, and he seems to welcome it." Briefly, I told the Barneses about what I had learned. They listened with terrified fascination. After my summary I wondered out loud, "Maybe I should turn all the evidence over to the authorities. They have the manpower to track down this evil-doer."

Mrs. Barnes tersely stated, "No, no more bungling police." Then her voice softened, "Are you frightened, James?"

I nodded, "Yes I am."

"You must realize if anyone is going to find this murderer, it's going to be you."

"Yes, I know."

"Mr. Barnes and I are somewhat sorry we brought you into this. God knows we don't want anything to happen to you. I'm afraid there is no turning back now."

She walked up to me, placing her hand on my shoulder. Her

tears almost made my knees buckle. With her husband standing beside her for support, she kissed me—holding her lips to the side of my mouth until I felt her cold tears on my cheek. When she pulled away, her face began changing, she said, "Don't let him get you, you are better than he is."

Her face now reverted entirely to its mournful, cold mask. It felt like this was her farewell to emotion. I looked from one to the other, saying, "I'll get him."

Mr. Barnes wrote out my weekly one thousand dollar check. Once again he walked me to the door, but this time following me all the way to the Wagoneer. I turned to say good-bye as he asked, "What will you do when you find him?"

"Turn him over to the police, I guess." He said nothing else. We shook hands and I left.

I raced back to the depths of Bridgeport and drove directly to my insurance man. I filled out a life insurance policy for half a million dollars. I made my insurance man so nervous, it took me half an hour to convince him I wasn't terminally ill. I needed to leave Sally and the girls well off just in case the killer got me.

When I entered the Stayawhile, I saw business was as good as the previous day, although my mood wasn't. However, I jumped behind the bar to help Georgie again. He yelled from the kitchen, "Two day in a row. Soon I got to pay you, but before that I let them all go fucking thirsty."

I worked my way down the bar to Harland, the biker. "You here again? Pretty soon I'll be seeing you playing pinochle with the old timers."

He laughed, offering a raspy-voiced greeting, "How goes it, man? Ye on top of the fuckin' world or what?"

"No, not really, Harland. I kind of had a bad day."

"Well, ye know what they say, man . . .'shit happens'. Don't

THE FOURTH ESTATE MURDERS

let it get ye down."

I placed the fresh glass of ale in front of him, saying, "Sorry about my friend yesterday."

"Oh, the cop? That ain't nothin'. Shit like that happens everyday."

"You mean the law harasses you?"

"What do ye think?"

He was probably right. Bikers looked so sloppy, yet intimidating in their garb. You had to wonder why they'd opt for such a life. What was even more baffling was why any of them would choose Bridgeport as their stomping grounds.

Harland finished his ale and said he thought that it would be better for us both if he left before Tommy came in. I think he was the first biker I met that I liked. It wasn't that he was different, because he was just like other bikers—he just seemed to be easier to talk to. After he'd left, I felt a little better about things.

I stayed behind the bar until Tommy arrived. I poured us each a beer and came around to greet him. After we sat down, he asked, "Alice wants to know when you are going to come over?"

"Never."

He laughed, "Well, if that's the case, you'd better tell her."

"Why does she always want me to come over?"

"She's worried about you. She says you are a lost, lonely soul."

"Oh yeah, and what's she going to do? Save me or something?"

"C'mon, Jimmy. You know she is concerned about you."

"Well, what the hell am I supposed to do? Act like her? Gather my daughters together every Sunday and go to church?"

He raised up his hands, "Hold it, Jimmy. What's wrong? Something happened today?"

I wasn't ready to tell him about the phone message or anything else I'd found out in the past twenty-four hours. Instead, as stupid as it seemed, I wanted to clear something up with him. "Tommy, do you remember maybe five or six years ago, having a game of one-on-one basketball?"

He chuckled, "If I tried I could remember a thousand games."

"No, no, this day you claimed you could play in the N.B.A. if you took the time to train. I didn't say it, but I felt the same way about baseball."

He looked at me like I was crazy. "So what the hell are you saying, Jimmy? That we should try out for pro basketball and baseball teams?"

No, I just want to know if you still think you could play pro ball?"

Now he gave me an incredulous look. "Have you lost your fuckin' mind? I'm forty years old, I've got a pile of kids, I'm going to retire in six or seven years. What the hell is the matter with you, Jimmy? Did Juju inflict brain damage on you?"

"Alright, alright, just forget about it. I'm sorry I even brought it up."

He put his hand on mine. He really was the brother I never had. "Listen, you stupid jerk. Wake up, our time has passed. Jeanie will be a teen this year. Let it go, Jimmy. It's all over. You are a private dick now, in more ways than one. Get into it and forget about freakin' baseball."

I knew he would continue to harp on it, so I abruptly changed the subject. "The killer called my answering machine."

Tommy listened while I told him the whole story, absolutely everything I had. He didn't interrupt once, which was unusual for him. When I finished speaking, he sat silent for a moment, then said, "Maybe you were right yesterday, we should have turned this over to the police."

THE FOURTH ESTATE MURDERS

"What about the reward, Tommy?"

"Yeah, I know. But what the hell good is the reward if you get killed?"

"I'm not going to get killed. I'll find him."

We talked a little longer with him asking me about Leslie, like if I had something special going on with her. I assured him that I didn't, yet he made me promise that I'd introduce him to her. That was Tommy, three little months older than me but always acting the role of the older brother. . . .

Leslie lived in a small apartment not far from my ex-wife and daughters. I knew the apartment building, having once had a girlfriend who lived there. As soon as she opened the door she began talking, "Did you hear? The Bridgeport Police caught James' murderer. I just received a call from my boss. They want me down there tomorrow morning at ten for a lineup. I hope this doesn't mean you'll have to leave anytime soon."

I looked around, almost every space on her walls was covered with a painting. "Hi, Leslie. No, I don't have to be anywhere. Can I use your phone for a minute?"

She nodded. I quickly called Tommy and informed him of what I had just learned, giving him Leslie's number so he could call me right back when he found out who the cops had.

When I hung up the phone she just stared at me. "You don't even sound like you believe they caught someone."

"Oh, no, that's not it. I'm sure they did, but they've probably got the wrong man."

She seemed to climb on a high horse and ride next to the high horse she thought I was on. "So you are that good a detective, are you?"

"No, Leslie, I don't mean to sound like that. It's not so much me being a good detective as it is the Bridgeport police being such bad detectives."

"I guess there is no need for me to even bother going down to the police station tomorrow morning."

"Probably not."

She was becoming upset, "I had you all wrong. I thought you were more of a lover boy than a know-it-all."

She tickled me with that one. "No, you had it right the first time."

I was saved by the phone bell. Tommy had already gotten the information. He told me who the police had nabbed, nothing else needed to be said. I hung up the phone and turned my attention back to Leslie. "I love these paintings. Are they all yours?"

Now her hands were on her hips, "Not so fast, Mr. Conte, who was that?"

"A friend on the Bridgeport police. He said the cops nabbed Alfredo Velez for the Walblont murder."

"You sound like you know him."

"I do, Leslie. He didn't kill our Mr. Walblont."

"How do you know?"

"Can we just forget about it? Here take this."

I handed her a bottle of wine I had brought with me. I shouldn't have put on that disdainful attitude. She was, no doubt, a little shaken up by the fact that she'd have to go down to identify this man tomorrow morning.

She took the wine, while offering an apology, "I didn't mean to call you a know-it-all. I'm sorry."

"Come on, let's just have a good time. I had a rough day myself."

That slight smile she seemed to have painted on her face became the focus of my attention. She asked, "Do you really like my work?"

She had everything hung up on her walls: pencil sketches,

water colors, oils— she was indeed an artist. I answered, "Yes, really. You're great. It seems a shame you should be wasting your time writing obituaries."

This I could see pleased her, but like a true artist she needed no more than that simple compliment. She changed the subject, "Well, I held true to my promise, it's shrimp with lobster sauce and fried rice."

"Sounds great."

I followed her into her kitchen. That was the whole apartment—the main room and a small kitchen. Between the two of our living quarters, it didn't amount to enough to satisfy one couple. The kitchen is where we ate the Chinese food, along with some of the wine. I told her all about growing up with Tommy and how, for the simple fact there were no other males around, we had became like brothers. She seemed really interested in my sports stories that almost always involved Tommy and, sometimes, even Juju.

When I finished she asked, "Is Tommy the same Tom you spoke to on the phone?"

"Yes, he's a desk sergeant down at the police station."

"Oh. How come he went on to become a police officer and you a private detective?"

"Well, you see, we both joined the police academy together, but I dropped out while Tommy stayed on to become the only cop I know who doesn't take graft."

"Why did you drop out?"

Everybody always had to ask me that. I simply gave the usual answer, "I didn't like it. So I figured I wouldn't have made a good cop."

When we returned to her main room, we just stood there for a moment. I asked, "What do we do now?"

She laughed out loud, "I don't know. You have any suggestions?"

"To use your words, you did call me a lover boy, you know."

"Forget it, Jimmy, it's not going to happen. Don't you ever do anything else with women besides sleep with them?"

"Yes, sometimes I argue with them, too."

"Well, you'll get no argument here, just a sock in the teeth."

"Oh, boy, I'm shaking all over."

We were standing looking at each other face to face, neither one of us knowing what to do until I asked, "How about a simple kiss to bond our friendship?"

"Ugh, that sounds so stupid. We're not children, you know."

I persisted, "I won't even put my tongue in your mouth."

"No, now stop it. You're making a fool of yourself."

"We won't even close our eyes and we won't move our heads, we'll just put our lips together for a brief moment."

"No, no, no."

"Please?"

She moved closer. "You are worse than a child, but if a stupid kiss means that much to you, you can have one."

Her face was lit up, showing off her natural good looks. She stood there in what looked to be a derisive pose, almost laughing. "Well, what are you waiting for? Let's get this over with."

"Thanks a lot, Leslie. You really know what buttons to push."

I didn't care. She could mock me all she wanted. I moved in, putting my arms around her. She sure was big and solid. I put my lips to hers, they were soft and felt inviting. Then she began to move them, she was getting excited. No, that wasn't it—she was giggling. Pulling away, I glanced at her face while she tried desperately to hold her laugh. I moaned, "You're a cruel person. No wonder your walls are completely covered with paintings. You have all this free time! Guys don't like to be laughed at when they're trying to kiss a girl."

It was just what she wanted to hear, she could hold her hilarity no longer. I felt like a fool.

It took a while, but she finally stopped snickering. We never left our embrace. Finally I said, "Okay, are you ready to try it again?"

Her giggling quickly subsided, "Are you insane?"

"Sure, I'm crazy and you are this woman who really knows how to treat a man."

She moved so close to me our bodies pressed against one another. "Aw, I hurt the little boy. I'm sorry. Let the meany Leslie make him all better." She began kissing me all over my face, my ears, my neck and my lips. I returned her kissing with my own. She offered no resistance until I tried to move her body closer to the couch. She was a big girl and this was no easy task. While I was trying to move her, our legs got tangled and we both fell to the floor. This ignited renewed laughter from Leslie. Out of control, she roared. I thought it was a little funny myself but I was more interested in figuring out a way to get to where we were before we fell.

Finally after she was all calmed down, she said, "Jim, I'm going to have to get some sleep. I'll need to be at work real early to do my job if I'm going to be at the police station by ten."

"You mean that's it? You're throwing me out?"

"Well, kind of, I guess."

This time when we kissed she practically pinned me to the wall. What a woman . . . but in no time I found myself outside, blinking my eyes and shaking my head.

I was tempted to call up Linda the Receptionist, but instead decided to go back to the office. As soon as I got inside the door, the phone began ringing. It was Leslie. Her voice sounded soft but sedate. "I just called to say good night. I hope you don't mind?"

"No, not at all. I was just thinking about what a crazy lady you are. I miss you already."

"Really? Good, because I miss you, too. I'm sorry I made you go."

"I can always come back."

"No, Jimmy, I've got to get some sleep. Will we see each other tomorrow?"

"I'll call you at work."

"You're a real good kisser, you know."

"Yeah, that's what you were thinking about when you were rolling around the floor, laughing."

She began to giggle again, recounting our zany kissing mishap. Eventually we said good night.

I was real tired. I did nothing to myself but undress and slip into bed. Outside the city was quiet as I drifted into sleep. Then a motorcycle engine began revving underneath my window, over and over again. The loud roars finally got me out of bed. I turned on the light and went to the window. Down below there was one lone biker who drove off as soon as he saw me. Cursing, I shut off the light and jumped back into bed.

Sleep returned a moment after my head hit the pillow. But shortly after that the phone rang again. I fumbled with the receiver wondering to myself if Leslie was one of those phone people. I answered as politely as I could, "Hello."

"Hey, man, how ye doin'? Did ye hear me outside your window? Bet I pissed ye off."

"Harland! Is that you?"

"Yeah, man. Who the fuck else?"

"How, how did you get my number?"

"Oh, c'mon, man, you're in the fuckin' book."

I was now wide awake. "You son-of-a-bitch. What do you want?"

THE FOURTH ESTATE MURDERS

"Whoooeee, bet ye'd like to take a swing at me now. Listen, man, I ain't gonna keep ye from your sleep. I know ye been lookin' for me real good. I just want to tell ye I got a big surprise for ye."

I was up off the bed, "It's you, isn't it? Where are you? I'll meet you right now."

"Shit man, ye can't be that fuckin' stupid. You're no match for me. Don't worry, man, you're safe; it's not you I'm after. C'mon now, Jimmy, ye know who I want."

"Newspaper people."

"Alright, man! I like your style. I'm gonna make sure ye got a ringside seat for the next one."

"Why does there have to be another one? Stop now. Nobody knows about you."

"Hey, man, c'mon now. Ye ain't going to try and spoil it, are ye?"

"I'll stop you, Harland."

"Shit, Jimmy. Ye and this whole fuckin' State Police Department couldn't stop me."

"Let's meet now, Harland."

"Ye got balls, Jimmy, I'll say that. But you're a fuckin' idiot. A stupid, low-life, third-rate, fuckin' idiot detective."

TEN

Paul Nelson's trailer was still at the Oak Tree Trailer Park, but he had moved into the St. Clair Boarding House in Stamford. During breakfast that morning, he enjoyed himself with many of the other boarding house guests. Some of the folks had lived there for years, some for months, or weeks and others, like himself, for only a few days.

After breakfast he returned to his small room with the Stamford Advocate. He immediately opened it to the sports section. He had hoped that eventually, when what he was doing was found out, journalist would take a more honest approach to their work. Using the periodicals to give the news was all well and good, but to use it as a forum for one's own self-serving motives was unforgivable. If the Fourth Estate would not properly weed out its incompetent journalists, then Paul Nelson would.

An article caught his eye. The headline read: "WOMEN SHOULD BOYCOT REMINGTON PRODUCTS". It was an article about Victor Kiam, the owner of Remington Shavers and professional football's New England Patriots. According to the story, female sportswriter Lisa Olsen allegedly claimed that while in the Patriot locker room, one of the players had insinuated that she seemed more interested in their genitals than in a story. Paul Nelson knew the whole affair had happened over four months ago but it never entirely left the newspapers. The truth of what really happened inside the locker room was never offered to the readers. Instead, the journalists took the side of Lisa Olsen, not because she was a woman, but because she was sports reporter, a member of the Fourth Estate.

Paul Nelson had read all about this occurrence, and as much as he didn't like Victor Kiam, it was nothing compared to his disdain for irresponsible journalism. When this event had first taken place, he had not yet decided to take action against the Fourth Estate. He had previously occupied himself with ridding the streets of the homeless. Now it was time to strike a major blow to the fraternity of journalists.

The article was written by a sportswriter named Gene Smith. Not only did he suggest that women should stop buying Remington shavers, but that the Commissioner of the National Football League should make Victor Kiam sell his interest in the Patriots.

Paul Nelson thought, *'He hass nothing to write about ssso he flingsss mud. We will give him a chance to retract, or we will deliver hisss corpsse to our new friend Jimmy.'*

Later that morning, Paul Nelson found a phone booth next to the Stamford Advocate. He rang up the sports department, claiming he was Victor Kiam's uncle. This ploy made it a simple matter to get to Gene Smith. When the sportswriter got on the phone, Paul Nelson introduced himself as Calvin Kiam. He spoke with the broad accent of a Bostonian. Gene Smith listened with patience while the "uncle" explained why he took offense to the article. After "Uncle Calvin" had said all he had to say, he asked Gene Smith to retract the article. But the columnist politely explained to the old man that this was the United States, and in this country we practiced freedom of press. Uncle Calvin tried to point out that if the roles had been reversed it wouldn't have mattered if Lisa Olsen was a woman or not, she still would have been chastised for offending a member of the press. After a few choice, four-letter words from Uncle Calvin, Gene Smith warned him that he'd hang up on him if he continued using vulgarity, and Smith finally did.

Paul Nelson called the newspaper three more times as Uncle Calvin and was finally told by the switchboard that Gene Smith had left for the day.

'Liess, more liess from the pressss. . . . '

The phone woke me up again; this time it was morning. My caller was my ex-wife, Sally. She said she needed to see me this afternoon and that it was very important. I tried to get it out of her what it was she wanted, but she said it would be better if I came over. She assured me everything was alright with the girls, basically that was all I cared about. I promised I'd be over sometime in the late afternoon.

I looked at the clock. It was already past eleven in the morning. After my last call from Harland, I had stayed up most the night trying to piece things together. There had to be a clue somewhere that I could grab a hold of. Somehow I thought Louie Rosselli might have some information. I would make it my business to see him real soon.

Tommy called. It was his day off. I told him about the call from Harland. He sounded shocked. When I said I needed to see Louie Rosselli today, he offered to come along. We agreed to meet in front of the Stayawhile in half an hour.

I was just about to walk downstairs when the phone rang again. The first words to penetrate my ear were, "You bastard! You horny, womanizing bastard!"

"Leslie, is that you?"

"Yes, it's me. You were right. The police arrested the wrong man. Do you know how they came to that conclusion?" She didn't give me a chance to answer. "I'll tell you how. I could

THE FOURTH ESTATE MURDERS

easily see they had the wrong man and if that wasn't enough proof, it was corroborated by Linda Kowalski. You know her? The blond receptionist at my paper? She told me all about your conversation at the Post building the morning after James was murdered. What are you up to, Jimmy? After my conversation with her, I put two and two together and realized that when I called up the Bridgeport Police to check on you, you told me to ask for Sergeant Thomas Harrington. Give me one reason why I shouldn't go to the police and tell them about you and your friend, Tommy?"

I could hear Tommy beeping his horn down in the street. "Listen, Leslie, I can explain everything. Please don't lose your trust in me."

She answered, "You are not the nice guy I thought you were, Jimmy Conte."

"Leslie, I've got to go. Can you come down to the Stayawhile Tavern at five o'clock this afternoon? I'll meet you in front of the place. We'll go up to my office and I'll explain everything."

"You've got a lot of nerve."

"Let's not overreact. Will you meet me there, please?"

"I'll meet you there, Jimmy, but I'm not making any promises."

That day Paul Nelson scanned through the telephone book and found seven Smiths whose first name was Gene. He began calling the Smiths until he got the home of Gene Smith, the sportswriter. To his delight the columnist was there. He spoke with a native New England accent, explaining to Gene Smith the sportswriter, that his name was also Gene Smith. The impostor told the columnist that he had received a telephone call from a woman who had erroneously taken him for Gene Smith, the sportswriter. She had spoken with such intensity and urgency in her voice that he hadn't had a chance to identify himself as the wrong Gene Smith, until it was too late.

Gene Smith, the sportswriter, expressed interest and coaxed the impostor to tell all. The impostor whispered into the phone that what the woman had said was not for the ears of his own wife and children, all of whom were at home. The sportswriter asked the impostor if he'd mind meeting him at a bar. The impostor, allowing his voice to sound meek and nervous, implied that he wouldn't feel comfortable in a public establishment. The sportswriter asked if he'd mind coming to his house. The impostor remained silent for a moment and then said he thought that would be the best idea. . . .

We drove through the east end of Bridgeport, probably the oldest section of the city and now, certainly, the most rundown. In the old days, the Mustaches had bosses from the cities of New York and Providence controlling Bridgeport. Nowadays that wasn't the case. It didn't seem like the big boys had much interest in Bridgeport anymore. Ever since Tony the Lung was killed (still unsolved), things had changed. Fat Mike was the top banana, but unlike Tony the Lung, he wasn't a member of one of the big crime families. So the Mustaches that worked for Fat Mike had only each other to protect their interests.

Tommy parked his station wagon right in front of the old factory building. The sign over the entrance read, Jenny's Famous Hot Dogs, Inc. He asked, "Did you bring your Beretta?"

"Yes, but that sort of thing won't be necessary. Just let me do the talking."

"Listen, Jimmy. If that dago mouths off once, he's going to be answering questions flat on his back."

"Maybe you should wait in the car."

"Come on, let's go."

THE FOURTH ESTATE MURDERS

As soon as we entered the building, the smell nearly dropped me to my knees. Tommy said, "What the hell are they making in here, wop cologne?"

"Ha, ha, real funny."

I asked a worker walking by with a empty hand truck where we could find Louie Rosselli. He pointed to the back of the building. As we walked to Louie's office, there was one thing I had become sure of. I would never eat another one of Jenny's Famous Hot Dogs ever again.

Louie's secretary must have been one of his relatives because she looked just like him, except she didn't have his thin mustache—hers was thick and greasy. When we asked to see Louie, she didn't even bother to announce us. She just pointed over her shoulder with her thumb saying, "He's right in dere."

We entered the office, finding Louie sitting down with his feet up on the desk, having himself a siesta. I tapped his foot, "Louie, wake up."

His body convulsed for a moment, then he looked up at Tommy and me. "What the fuck are you doin' in here?"

"Hi, Lou. Sorry I had to wake you up."

"Get the fuck outta here before I have both yer legs broken."

"Calm down, Lou. I just need to ask you a few more questions, okay?"

Tommy entered the conversation, "Yeah, Mr. Rosselli. Why don't you just answer his questions and we'll be out of your hair?"

Louie got up from behind his desk and walked toward us, speaking as he did, "Who the fuck is the mick, Jimmy? What are you doin', fuckin' this potato head up the ass, er what?"

Tommy was all over him. In a few seconds Louie was down on his back with Tommy on top, choking him. I didn't want to get involved. I knew Tommy wouldn't kill him, at least I thought he wouldn't. I looked down, Louie was gasping for air while the back of Tommy's neck was a rich pinkish-red. "Alright, Tom. That's enough. Come on, Tommy, Louie's my friend. Right Lou?"

Louie's eyes were bulging out of his face as he nodded his head that indeed he was my friend. Tommy placed his hand over Louie's mouth and then took a bite out of his shoulder while Louie kicked in pain. Then he put his face right in front of Louie's saying, "When I let you up, don't say one freakin' word until you're asked a question. You got that, you fuckin', greasy, slimeball guinea."

They both got up off the floor. Louie was about to speak, but Tommy pointed a finger at him and he quickly clammed up. Even though the smell wasn't as bad inside Louie's office as it was outside, it was giving me a sick stomach. I wanted to leave real bad. I was going to make this quick. "Why did you tell me Juju killed Morgan Barnes when you knew he didn't?"

He looked at Tommy to see if it was okay for him to speak. Tommy nodded it was. He answered, "Jesus, Jimmy, this is fuckin' crazy."

Tommy yelled, "Answer his question, squid face."

"Alright, alright. I wasn't sure. Juju could've killed the guy."

"Do you know a black man named Robin Harris?"

"Yeah, I know him."

"How?"

"Believe me, Jimmy, that fuckin' nigger ain't got nothin' to do with this."

"How do you know?"

"'Cause I hired him to clean up the apartment building so I could get that scum-bag Barnes off my back before he put me out of business."

"Where does Harris live?"

THE FOURTH ESTATE MURDERS

"I don't know. He came and he went."

"Just like that, he walked in the door one day?"

"No, not like that. My ex-sister-in-law, Blanche Herman recommended him."

"Why?"

"Ah, she's got a trailer park out in Southport. I guess he asked her if she knew where he could get some work. She always sends people to me. She talks 'bout me all the time. She thinks I'm a fuckin' bank."

"What's the name of the trailer park?"

"Oak Tree Trailer Park of Southport. But I'm telling you, the fuckin' nigger's a nice guy. He cleaned up the first floor real good, I paid him, bingo—he was outta here. It wasn't Harris who offed Barnes, it was that *eggplant*, Juju."

I turned around and walked out; Tommy followed. We left Louie standing there speechless, that is until Tommy was out of earshot.

Tommy was attempting to ask me questions, but all I could think about was getting out of the hot dog factory. We burst out onto the street. It was the first time Bridgeport ever smelled good. I took in some of the free air, hoping it would relieve my churning stomach. Instead it caused great eruptions from within. Leslie's Chinese food from the previous night suddenly regurgitated, and was now the welcome mat at the entrance of Jenny's Famous Hot Dogs.

When we got back inside Tommy's station wagon, he put on the air-conditioner even though it was the middle of the winter. He asked, "You okay, Jimmy?"

I felt much better, but I thought if I saw a hot dog I'd get sick all over again. I answered, "Yeah, I'm alright. Get up on the turnpike and let's go to Southport."

Tommy sounded like he was up for this, "You got it, kid."

ED CALANDRO

In some ways it was nice to be a cop. You could break the simple laws, like speeding and running lights. He shut off the air-conditioner and drove to the East Main Street entrance to the turnpike. I was a little annoyed, "Tommy, was it necessary to be so rough on Louie?"

"Don't worry about it, Jimmy, he's only a greaseball."

"Yes, and that also. Has it ever occurred to you that I'm Italian, too?"

He placed both hands on the steering wheel and looked at me with shock all over his face. "No! You mean you're a greasy, dago, guinea, white-flag-waving, ass-pinching, midget, bird-eating, almost-black, garlic-breath, squid-faced wop?"

Tommy had such a way with words. I looked out of my window. As soon as you get out of the city limits of Bridgeport, the state becomes New England again. We were only fifteen minutes away from Southport. I took the time to think about Leslie. I wondered if she and Linda had talked about other things besides the James Walblont murder. . . .

Paul Nelson chose to disguise himself as a tattered, middle-aged businessman—dirty-blond wig, glasses, rumpled sports jacket, blue shirt with tie. The St. Clair Boarding House was practically empty during the afternoon; those who remained there were either napping, reading, or watching television. He climbed out of the window of the boarding house and wheeled his motorcycle to the end of the parking lot. The directions to his house the sportswriter had given him, were precise. Paul Nelson cruised by on his Yamaha, then drove away, parking nearly five blocks from the house. Soon after, he hailed a cab which took him to the front door of the sportswriter's home.

At the front door, the two Gene Smiths introduced themselves, then the impostor meekly following the sportswriter inside. The

THE FOURTH ESTATE MURDERS

house was circa the early nineteen hundreds with the decor underscoring the era. Gene Smith led the impostor into the living room where he sat down on a comfortable chair. The sportswriter asked, "Would you care for coffee or tea?"

Paul Nelson timidly answered, "No, thank you. I'd like to get this over with as quickly as possible, if you don't mind."

This prompted Gene Smith to close the double doors that led into the rest of the house. He sat down on a chair opposite his guest.

Paul Nelson folded his hands in his lap thinking . . . *'No finger printsss.'* He could hear that there were other people in the house. He wished to get his business finished with as soon as he could, so he asked, "May I begin?"

Gene Smith replied eagerly, "Please do."

The impostor whispered, "The woman who called, mistaking me for you, identified herself to me but made me give my word I wouldn't divulge her identity. When I explained to her that she had confided in the wrong Gene Smith, she became so hysterical that I felt it necessary to give her some comfort by saying I would help her. But I must tell you, even though I know how to get in touch with her, for the time being we'd like to keep her identity a secret. I hope that is acceptable to you?"

The sportswriter, eager to hear, yet annoyed that this other Gene Smith was already holding back information, reluctantly nodded his agreement.

The impostor continued his story, "Once she had named herself and was sure she could trust me, she said she had learned six months past that her husband was a homosexual."

Gene Smith, still a little annoyed, cut in, "Why would she want to tell me? I'm a sports columnist. She should call a lawyer."

Paul Nelson sat quietly for a moment, then whispered, "Because her husband and his lover are members of a New York professional baseball team."

The columnist sat stunned, while the impostor thought. . . . *'Look at hisss mouth watering.'*

Gene Smith asked anxiously, "Which team, Yanks or Mets?"

The impostor answered, "It is not for me to say. But there is much more. She had witnessed the seduction of a shortstop prospect by her husband and a highly placed office official during spring training. Later on she learned that the young prospect finally refused to do things with them any longer and so was promptly shuttled back down to the minor leagues."

Paul Nelson noticed the demon-like interest of Gene Smith— *'I've got him.'*

He had learned from the many roles he played never to go too far with the guise, yet he couldn't help but play off his unsuspecting co-stars. And in Gene Smith he had a provocative subject. He continued, playing like a cat might with a trapped mouse. "There are also the bat boys." He hesitated for a moment, clearing his throat, and bowing his head in shame, bringing his voice to the softest of whispers, "They get them from one of those man\child organizations. They tell the rest of the team the bat boys come from camp contests."

The sportswriter sat in complete awe. This is what it was all about. Finding out the truth. "I need names and proof. I need to meet this person. Help me, Mr. Smith? Help me to put a stop to this decadence."

The impostor thought for a moment, then whispered, "I'll help you, but I want to be left out of it completely. Do you agree?"

Gene Smith looked confused, "But why?"

"Because I have a family. This isn't the sort of thing I want them exposed to. So if you want my help, you will not try and contact me or use my name in any way. Agreed?"

THE FOURTH ESTATE MURDERS

The sportswriter knew that, for the time being, he had better play along with this timid dullard. So he concurred. As they walked to the front door together, the imposter made sure the only thing he touched with his hands was the outstretched hand of Gene Smith. He hurriedly walked down the sidewalk before the columnist could ask where his car was. . . . '*I musst work fasst before he triesss to look up all the Gene Ssmithsss in the telephone book.* . . .'

We pulled into the Oak Tree Trailer Park, having driven almost the whole way without talking. Tommy parked his station wagon near a trailer with an "Office" sign out front. Before we got out, I said, "This time let me do all the talking."

"Forget it, Jimmy, I'm the police officer here."

"Yes, I know, that's why I want to do the talking."

"What's that supposed to mean?"

"Nothing, just don't say anything or punch her in the mouth or anything like that. Okay?"

He chortled, "Touchy, aren't we?"

In our lifetime, Tommy and I had more arguments and fights than I wish to remember. In the past three or four years I had learned that the best way to contend with him was to ignore him.

I walked up to the front door of the trailer, knocking before Tommy had a chance to catch up to me. Shortly, a middle-aged woman answered, "Yes, good afternoon. Can I help you?"

"Hi, I'm sorry to bother you. We're looking for Blanche Herman."

"I'm Mrs. Herman. How may I help you?"

"My name is Jim Conte and this is Tom Harrington. We're friends of your brother-in-law, Louie Rosselli."

"Oh! Friends of Louis. Won't you come in?"

We followed her inside to her tiny living room. "Please have a seat. Would you care for some homemade chocolate chip cookies?"

I shook my head no, but Tommy said, "Please, I'd love some. We haven't had anything to eat today."

She dropped some cookies on a plate, saying, "Did Louis tell you he was married to my poor sister, Imogene? They were so happy. Too bad she died so young. Now Louis is all alone. He's such a nice man, isn't he?"

Tommy and I looked at one another. He giggled, "He sure is, I was just recently trying to make him understand how I feel about him."

She placed the cookies in front of Tommy and sat down next to me. "Well, now, what can I do for you two fine gentlemen?"

I smiled, "We were hoping you might be able to tell us how to get in touch with Robin Harris."

"Oh, yes, you mean the black man I sent to Louis."

"Yes, ahem, Louis said that he did such a fine job that we thought, possibly, he'd like to come and work for us."

"Dear me, I'm sure he would. Mr. Nelson said he has such a large family to feed."

Tommy was quick to inquire, "Who's Mr. Nelson?"

"He lives in one of the trailers here. He recommended Mr. Harris to me."

I stood up, "Well, then, maybe it's Mr. Nelson we should be talking to."

"Gosh, I'm afraid that's quite impossible, you see Paul, I mean Mr. Nelson, is away on business. I don't expect him back for five or six more days."

Tommy and I looked at each other, while he munched on a cookie, asking, "All we need is Robin Harris' telephone number, anyway. If you could provide us with that, we could contact him ourselves?"

THE FOURTH ESTATE MURDERS

"Oh, dear, I'm afraid that's quite impossible, too. You see, Paul has his number. But if this isn't an emergency, if you can wait until Mr. Nelson returns, I know he would love to help find work for Mr. Harris."

Tommy joined me standing, shrugging his shoulders, "Then we'll wait until Mr. Nelson returns."

Blanche Herman walked us back outside. She told us that Mr. Nelson and she were discussing the possibility of becoming partners in the Oak Tree Trailer Park. She even hinted that there may be a little romance in the air. To hear her talk, Paul Nelson was Prince Charming.

We were in front of Tommy's station wagon. The cold winds of winter twisted and turned all around us. It seemed strange how we were only fifteen minutes away from Bridgeport, yet the air could be so fresh. I extended my hand to Blanche Herman, "Thank you so much. I guess we'll just have to wait until Mr. Nelson returns."

She nodded, "Yes. Paul will be more than happy to put you in touch with Mr. Harris."

Tommy seemed to be thinking exactly what I was, saying, "This is a great little trailer park."

"Oh, thank you."

It was my turn, "Which one is Mr. Nelson's?"

She pointed, "It's that Airstream by the woods."

I looked at the silver-colored trailer. "That's a nice one. . . ."

Back on the turnpike Tommy asked, "So what do you think, partner?"

"I don't know, Tom. I've got a bad feeling about this Robin Harris, but we're going to have to wait until her boyfriend, Paul Nelson, returns."

"How about him?"

"Yeah, who knows. He might have something to do with it. I think one of us should take a ride out here every day just to make sure he hasn't returned yet."

"You're right, it's better than calling her, just in case he's dirty, it might scare him off."

Tommy had the radio on so softly that I could barely hear the music playing, but the song was so identifiable. I turned up the volume. It was "Release Me" by the all-girl trio, Wilson Phillips. He looked at me, confused, "What the hell are you doing, Jimmy?"

"It's this song, Tommy. I love this song. I feel like it was written for me."

He yelled, "My daughters listen to this group. This freakin' music is for kids."

"I know it. Jeanie gave me the tape. She said, Daddy listen to these girls sing, they make me think of you."

"Oh, right. How about if she asked you to listen to Big Bird and that stupid-ass frog doing a duet. What the hell would you do then—buy yourself a rubber ducky?"

Tommy could be so insensitive. He had no idea how I felt about this musical group.

When we got to the Stayawhile, I looked at my watch. It was already close to four in the afternoon. I had promised Sally I'd come up to see her, but Leslie would also be here in an hour. I asked Tommy if he wouldn't mind meeting Leslie here, just in case I wasn't back in time. I told him to bring her into the Stayawhile and treat her nicely. He agreed to do so, but was upset that I thought I had to tell him how to treat a lady—him having five daughters of his own. . . .

Later that afternoon Paul Nelson called Gene Smith's home only to find out that he had returned to work at the Stamford

THE FOURTH ESTATE MURDERS

Advocate. The switchboard at the paper promptly gave him Gene Smith's extension. "Yes, hello. Gene Smith speaking."

The impostor spoke in that timid tone he had used at the reporter's house. "Hello, Mr. Smith." He giggled softly, "This is the other Gene Smith."

The sportswriter immediately acknowledged, "Yes, sir, Mr. Smith, I've been thinking about you all afternoon. I was about to start calling up all the other Gene Smiths in the telephone book. I'm becoming anxious, but I did give my word. How have you made out?"

"I have been in touch with the woman we spoke of earlier. She wishes to meet you as soon as possible."

The sportswriter replied, "Good, good. When can we meet?"

"She said she'll be waiting near the front gate of St. Vincent's Hospital in Bridgeport. Do you know where it is?"

The columnist answered enthusiastically, "Yes, I do."

"She's asked that you come alone. She says she's uncertain what she should do until she talks to you. Is that okay?"

"Sure, that's fine. Will you be with her?"

The impostor growled, "No, Mr. Smith. I must beg off. This has already been much too trying for me."

"Okay. Well, er, what's her name?"

"She'll tell you her name. She won't be difficult to find. She said she will have on a grey suit on. She has dark hair and is rather attractive. I wish you luck, and do hope you are able to help her. Remember your promise to leave me out of all this."

"Don't worry, Mr. Smith, you'll never be mentioned in print, at least not by this writer, and thank you."

Paul Nelson drove back to the St. Clair Boarding House. He would need these few precious hours to prepare for his date with the inquisitive Mr. Smith. . . .

I pulled up to my house, or Sally's—depending on whom is to be believed, me or the judge who awarded it to her. Before I even shut off the engine, all three were out to greet me. I got out of the Wagoneer and opened my arms. First Sara jumped into them, planting kisses all over my face. "Take it easy, honey, you're acting like you haven't seen me for years."

"I love you, Daddy."

"I love you too, baby." I released her and Jeanie immediately walked into my embrace. Again I was struck by her girlish makeup, "Hi, Dad."

"Hello, princess. What have I done to deserve such a greeting?" I bent down slowly, as she put her arms around my neck and kissed me.

"You didn't do anything, Daddy, except be who you are, and for that we will always love you."

I had always been a pushover for my daughters' compliments, but I wasn't stupid. "What's going on?"

Jeanie, who usually looked me directly in the eyes, turned away a little, asking, "Daddy, Sara and I want to see you this weekend, is that alright?"

"Of course, you don't have to go through this to ask."

"Can we stay at your office, like we did when you and Mommy first got divorced?"

"I guess, if you want to."

She clapped her hands, smiling at me. "Goody. Sara and I are going to Jillian's house for a while." She kissed me again on the cheek and then off they went with Sara yelling, "Bye, Daddy."

I glanced at my ex with her arms folded, proudly watching our two daughters scamper off to the neighbor's house. "Hi, Sally. That sure was a strange greeting."

She wasted no time. "Jimmy, I have someone inside I'd like you to meet."

"Who?"

"His name is Blake Lennon."

"What's he want?" She turned and started walking for the front door. I asked again, "Who the hell is Blake Lennon?"

She spun around, staring directly at me. "If you'll wait for one goddam minute, you'll find out."

I followed her inside, through the living room and into the kitchen. There was a thin man with curly gray hair, dressed in drab clothes. He was preparing something at the kitchen counter.

Sally spoke quickly, not wanting me to get in the first words. "Jimmy, I'd like for you to meet my friend, Blake Lennon."

He turned around with hand extended. He seemed a little young to have so much gray hair. I put out my hand to shake, he smiled and took it. "So, what's the big deal, Sally? You introduce me to one of your boyfriends. What am I supposed to do? I know you have male guests."

She interrupted, "Jimmy, stop it! Why don't you sit down?"

I looked at her skinny boyfriend. He stared back, offering no hostility. I never took my eyes off him, answering her, "I don't want to sit down. Why don't you have a seat?"

Blake Lennon interrupted, "I was just boiling a pot of water. Would you care for a cup of mint tea, Mr. Conte?"

Sally walked in between us. "Oh hell, Blake, call him Jimmy."

She turned to me, there was fear on her face. I didn't know if she thought I was going to hurt her or if she was going to hurt me. "Jimmy, Blake's moving in here."

For a moment I could hear nothing else except for a dull ringing in my ears. I could think of nothing challenging to say except, "This is my house."

Sally replied in the same hollow tone, "No, it isn't."

Blake walked out from behind the counter, closer to me. "I know it's your house, Mr. Conte. Sally talks about you all the time. She has told me how hard you work for her and your daughters. I can't imagine what it must be like for you to meet a man moving into your house with your wife and children."

I sat down and looked at Sally. "What about the girls?"

"They know, Jim. They're growing up. They want me to have a life of my own. Their main concern is you."

I looked at Blake Lennon and pointed at the counter, "What are you making over there?"

He smiled, "It's just a salad, would you care to join us?"

"No, thanks, I guess you're a vegetarian, too?"

"Absolutely, wouldn't have it any other way."

I chuckled, "At least I won't have to come up here in the summer time and mow the lawn anymore. You and Sally can go out there and graze on it."

She frowned while her boyfriend laughed uproariously. I did have a cup of mint tea. Blake had a house of his own and was going to rent it. He explained that they had agreed I would only have to make half the mortgage payment while their cohabitation continued. He said that he had met Sally at the Green Earth Health Food Store quite a while ago. Sally had talked about me so much, he didn't realize for almost six months that we were divorced. I didn't know if he was attempting to flatter me or if he was just jealous. Either way, he was a pretty honest, nice guy.

Sally walked me out to the Wagoneer. "So what do you think, Jimmy?"

"I think you lucked out, Sal."

She put her arm around me, beaming. "Really?"

I put my arm around her as we continued walking, "Yeah, yeah. What do you want me to do, say he's better than me?"

She stopped walking, looking at me. She had the cutest, most sincere face. "No, Jimmy. I could never think that, Blake knows that. We are both on the rebound. His wife ran off with a classical guitar player, while my husband ran off with half the female population."

Sally's eye's were wet. She turned and ran inside. I got into the Wagoneer and headed for the Stayawhile. I believe my eyes got a little wet themselves. . . .

That evening after he finished some work at the Stamford Advocate, Gene Smith stopped at Sammy's—a favorite watering hole for members of the Fourth Estate. A short time later, with the aid of a few Dewar's and sodas in him, the reporter began hinting to his colleagues that he was on to something big. Not all journalists favored Gene Smith's tactics, as they were keenly aware he'd do just about anything for a story. The fact that he claimed to be onto something big peaked the curiosity in a few of his closest cronies.

Dave Feldman and Mick McManis, two rival sportswriters, latched onto Gene Smith. He had sensed their interest, and, yes, allowed them to buy him more scotch and soda. After Dave Feldman bought another round, he urged, "Come on, Geno, what gives? What's going down?"

Gene Smith half smiled because of the story that was about to come forth, and also because a few Dewars always made him smile. Micky McManis slurred, "It must be out and out nasty if Geno won't even give us a hint."

Gene Smith looked at his two bloodshot-eyed friends and whispered, "It's much more than nasty." Then in a louder voice he offered, "It's loathsome!"

Micky and Dave were duly impressed. But they were even more concerned that their buddy Geno kept looking at his wristwatch. Finally Gene Smith put his arms around his two pals, saying, "Got to go, amigos. Duty calls." And the reporter, half drunk, rolled out of Sammy's. Unbeknownst to him, his two buddies had already decided to follow. . . .

Paul Nelson had just finished shaving his legs from the calves all the way to the ankles. Periodically during the early evening he had also shaved his face a few times, even though practically no facial hair grew there. It had become time to apply his makeup. He had an old photograph of Ava Gardner, one of his favorites, and he would use her face to help design his own. The high cheekbones and the classic look were what he was after. When he had finished, he was sure he had achieved his goal. He strapped his bra over two wholesomely-made, foam-rubber cups. He covered them with a white-on-white blouse and a black lace tie. Next he put on an attractive, gray, suit jacket. He placed his heels, skirt, light gray gloves, wig, and purse all in a large paper bag. He pulled an oversized sweatshirt over the gray jacket and pulled the hood over his head, then grabbed the paper bag and quietly sneaked out the window of the St. Clair Boarding house.

Driving down a country road he had previously sought out, he rode his Yahama almost to the Bridgeport city line. He put on his skirt, heels, wig and gloves. Her reached inside his purse and took out a mirror and lipstick. After he had applied just the right amount, he approved of his makeup with an attractive feminine smile. He-who-was-now-a-she dropped the mirror and lipstick back inside the purse and grabbed an old reliable perfume called "Evening Enchantment", putting on just enough to be seductive, careful not to over do it.

She hid her motorcycle under some brush, walked out to the main road and down to the corner bus stop. There she eventually caught a bus destined for St. Vincent's Hospital. . . .

Leslie edged her Dodge slowly down the curbside of Main

Street. She saw the sign identifying the Stayawhile, but there was no Jimmy anywhere. Then she noticed a short, stocky, blond-haired man walking toward her. He yelled, "Miss Van Houten, park the car. I'm Jimmy's friend."

She braked the little Honda and shut off the ignition.

Tommy opened the door for her. "Hi, I'm Tommy Harrington."

She got out of the car and shook his hand. "Oh, yes. Jimmy's sergeant friend. We've spoken on the phone."

"Yeah, he told me how upset you were. I'm sorry about that."

"What are you boys up to now?"

Tommy pointed to the front door of the Stayawhile. "Do you want to go inside? I'll explain what I can."

She nodded, "I guess. Jimmy has spoken of this place, but it's so seedy-looking."

Tommy laughed, "If you think it looks bad from out here, wait until we go inside."

He opened the door and she walked in, already liking Jimmy's friend.

They sat down in one of the booths while Georgie brought over two beers. Tommy seemed to be giving her a knowing smile. She asked, "What? What's the matter? You seem to know something that I don't."

"No, it's not that. I'm just being stupid; don't pay any attention to me."

"Well, then, what were you doing?"

His face turned red, "I was just kind of welcoming you into our lives, ever since I figured out that Jimmy was falling for you."

"Oh, dear. You are abrupt, aren't you?"

Tommy went on to tell Leslie all about Jimmy, including the facts of Jimmy being hired privately to find the Barnes killer. But he didn't go too far into detail about this because he didn't want to betray Jimmy, nor did he wish to lie to her if he could avoid it.

She liked Tommy—he was just as Jimmy had said, and she was glad he obviously liked her. He went on to say how Jimmy had gone from woman to woman ever since he and Sally had gotten their divorce. He had known almost immediately that something was going on with Leslie by the way Jimmy spoke of her, and he told her so now.

Leslie, who had been extremely hurt all day, was now feeling greatly relieved. There was also a comfortable feeling that she had with Tommy which allowed her to ask freely, "Why did you finish the Police Academy and Jimmy didn't?"

He ran his fingers through his hair. "Everybody asks that question, all the time. We always lie. He says whatever he feels like and I say whatever I want, too."

"Is there any chance I'll hear the truth?"

"Yeah, but I'm not going to tell Jimmy I told you."

"Why wouldn't you?"

"Because he isn't going to like it."

Tommy looked out toward the bar to make sure no one was sitting close enough to hear them. When he was satisfied, he began, "You see, after Jimmy and I got out of high school, we both got scholarships to universities. I went to U.B. here in Bridgeport and Jimmy went to the University of Miami on a baseball scholarship. I never made it through the first semester. My grades were too low. Jimmy did better—he lasted two full years, but he and his baseball coach never got along. So without any warning, Jimmy dropped out of school after his sophomore year.

"We didn't see much of Jimmy for a while after that. Before he went away he was a tough guy around here. He used to get into fights all the time . . . but when he came back home, he had changed. Wherever he went, whatever he did—no one knew, but Jimmy was a different person. He hadn't become a wimp or anything like that. As a matter of fact, to me the change was for the better.

"So anyway, I got Jimmy a job at the factory I was working in at that time. He wasn't there more than three weeks before he announces he's going to take the police test and urges me to do the same. We both pass, and the next thing you know we're in the Police Academy. So now we're both doing real great, the commander of the school even inquires about Jimmy going to a local school and getting a degree in criminology. Then one day the crap hits the fan. We had our pistols for three or four days, breaking them down and cleaning them, that sort of stuff. So now we have our first day of target practice. I didn't see Jimmy for most of the day, except near the very end. He had just gotten out of the shower. I asked him how he did. He looks me right in the eyes and tells me he's dropping out of the academy. Just like that. I tried everything to talk him out of it, but before we left that day, Jimmy quit.

"On the drive back home I'm real mad, cursing and yelling at him. He doesn't care; it's like he's not even paying attention to me. Then I stop the car and ask him what's wrong. He doesn't say anything for a while, then right out of left field he says, 'I can't do it, I can't shoot anyone. I couldn't even aim at those stupid targets with the phony faces on them'."

Tommy stopped talking for a moment, then said to Leslie, "Jimmy's coming in. . . ."

Gene Smith was slightly drunk when he got into his car in the rear parking lot of Sammy's. And it was because of that trifling drunkenness that he didn't notice his two colleagues, Dave

Feldman and Micky McManis, following as discreetly as possible. It was that way as Gene Smith merged onto the Merritt Parkway, the easiest route to Bridgeport and St. Vincent's Hospital. While he drove he thought about how soon everybody would be talking about him, not only in Connecticut—but all over the nation. Of course he'd have to implicate the other Gene Smith, there was no way he could avoid it. The man had seemed timid enough and probably would never trust another newspaper person, so there was no need to think there would be an opportunity for him to tell his side of the story. Plus the reporter thought he'd make a point of telling the other Gene Smith that it was the wife of the ballplayer who had originally involved him. That allowed the semi-drunk sportswriter a laugh because in his pocket he already had the telephone book page with all the other Gene Smiths on it. So, by the time the night was over, he would have not only the full story, but he would also be the first to get a statement from the other Gene Smith.

But first the woman. He wondered if he knew her. He'd enjoy seeing her squirm. As far as he was concerned, players' wives were useless. There were times when players would rather go home to their wives and tell *them* a story instead of telling him. And that was something he just could not understand. . . .

Micky McManis was trying to stay at least two cars behind Gene Smith and was, for the most part, doing a fine job. Dave Feldman asked, "Do you think that maybe Geno is pulling our cranks?"

"No way, he's got a story alright. Or maybe. . . ? No, it couldn't be that."

"What, Mick? What?"

"Maybe he's got a woman, you know, a girlfriend. Could he possibly be cheating on Ethel?"

THE FOURTH ESTATE MURDERS

Dave Feldman laughed, "I hope not, but whatever, I think this is going to be one hell of an evening."

Micky swerved out into the passing lane, then back in. Two cars behind his buddy Geno, fine driving indeed. . . .

Paul Nelson had been waiting at the front gate of the hospital for almost twenty minutes. It was at times like these that shear bliss would overwhelm him. The sensation of standing at such a popular walkway and not being noticed for who he was gave him a feeling of divine power. Except for a few men offering him a second complimentary look, he went unnoticed. He thought that if this small prelude to drama brought him joy, then what was coming next would, no doubt, bring jubilation. The date with this member of the Fourth Estate is what really got him going.

His gift of disguise and deception was only a small part of it. The whole world was his theater. His life, his being was dedicated to his on-going performance. He was, and he knew it, the only really pure actor; not to mention director, playwright, makeup person—the whole works. But most of all he was the actor of the future. Whenever he'd play himself in a role such as the one he was in now, a feeling of euphoria would momentarily take hold of him. It was almost what he thought death would be like. His whole life would pass before him, his eyes would half shut and he'd whirl through this life he was living. But in the truest sense of professionalism, he would pull himself together and proceed with the matter at hand. He had learned his craft thoroughly so why not use it for the good of all mankind? Why not use his gift to eliminate those who would try to distort what really was, into what they thought would be more interesting. . . .

Gene Smith pulled up to the curb nearest the front gate of St. Vincent's. He leaned over to the passenger side and rolled down the window. "Excuse me, ma'am. My name is Gene Smith. Ahem, might you be the lady I'm supposed to be meeting?"

Paul Nelson took a few dainty steps toward the car window. He felt the great challenge of acting surge through his being. In the disguise of a ballplayer's wife, the transition from man to woman took hold. There was a slight look of worry on her face as she walked to the sportswriter's car—yet not enough to lose the sensuality she was trying to convey. With the mind of a woman she allowed the prey to think he was the predator.

Gene Smith realized that he didn't know this baseball player's wife. He quickly ran through his head all the players wives he didn't know. But that was too difficult; after all, the scotch still owned part of his mind. For a moment they just stared. Then he asked, "Would you like for me to park the car, or do you wish to get in?"

She reached for the door handle and, with the help of the columnist, opened it. As she entered, her fragrance preceded her. The sportswriter felt a little uncomfortable, but also felt good. His curiosity, though, was damaging his rational thought. Who was the husband of this classy-looking broad? "Well, I've already said my name, and I assure you I am the Gene Smith you have been looking for all along. . . ." *'Yesss I know.'*

The reporter began to fidget a little, "And you are Mrs. . . ?"

She turned her head slightly toward her prey and in a soft feminine voice asked, "Can we please go?"

The confused sportswriter replied, "Go! Go where? And what is your name?"

"Mr. Smith, please be patient. I'll tell you my name shortly, but first we must discuss a few matters. Please drive on, I'll tell you when to turn."

Gene Smith thought, what the hell! The scotch, the perfume and probably the best story of my career—I might as well play along. . .

Micky and Dave watched as their buddy Geno's car pulled away from the curb. The Mick spoke quickly, "I told you, Davy. He's fucking cheating on Ethel."

Dave Feldman was not entirely convinced, "Follow him, Micky. Follow him."

"But Davy, it's none of our business."

"Follow him, Micky. If Geno was cheating, he wouldn't be bragging about a big scoop. Unless of course his dick is doing the thinking for him these days."

Micky laughed as he pulled out and quickly caught up to a safe distance behind his crony, Geno Smith. . . .

As soon as I entered the Stayawhile I saw that Tommy was obviously doing a fine job of entertaining Leslie. I had been expecting the worst from her. Now that I was also late, I had no idea how she would act. Tommy greeted me first, "Hey, buddy. How'd everything go?"

I nodded to him and quickly turned to her, "I'm sorry I'm late, Leslie. It couldn't be helped."

Tommy interrupted, "So what happened? Is Sally okay?"

"Yes, she's fine. She wanted me to meet her boyfriend, he's moving into the house."

Tommy's face reddened, "Did you have a blow-up?"

Leslie slid over allowing me to sit down next to her. "No, he was alright. He looks like he doesn't eat enough Trail Mix, but he's a nice guy."

Georgie brought me over a beer, "Hey, Jimmy, how you do?"

"I'm okay, Georgie. Thanks."

"Is this you new lady friend Tommy say you hot for?"

I gave Georgie an annoyed look, then glanced at Tommy and Leslie. He must have fixed things with her because they were both smiling. "Georgie, why don't you go stick your head inside the oven again."

He walked off, agreeing, "That not bad idea."

Tommy always had something to say, and for the short time that I had spent with Leslie, I found her to be the same way. But now, neither one said anything. I took a swallow of my beer while both of them watched me. They were getting me nervous. "Come on! What's up? I'm okay, really. Christ, we've been divorced for two years. Believe me, I'm not upset."

Leslie reached for my hand underneath the table. She was trying to comfort me. In a way, it was kind of a blessing. At least I wouldn't have to squirm and apologize for the way I had deceived her.

Tommy asked, "So, what now?"

"Leslie and I are going out to have a good time."

She squeezed my hand, "Jimmy, I can't. I know we had a date, but I have to break it. My mother has been sick for quite some time now. I made arrangements to pick up my brother in Waterbury and we are going to drive up to Hartford to see her."

With her holding my hand and all, I kind of thought we might have a romantic evening. Tommy showed off his gleaming, Irish smile, "Don't worry, Jimmy, I'll stay with you, Alice and the girls went to a show at the school."

With her free hand, Leslie grabbed Tommy's hand, "Oh, will you Tom. That would be so nice."

"Hey! What is this? Am I some kind of child or something? I can take care of myself just fine."

Leslie gave me a sidelong glance, "Yes, I'm sure you can. There is always Linda the Receptionist." She squeezed my hand tight, digging her nails into it. "I think you and Tom should have a nice, friendly dinner together and as this evening progresses, remember to say favorable remarks about me. If for no other reason than the fact that I've decided not to ask any more questions about exactly what kind of investigation you two are carrying on."

Tommy vowed, "Leslie, during the course of the evening I pledge to express my gratitude and pleasure that you have come into our lives and have already forgiven us for our lying ways."

The three of us talked for a little while longer. It seemed like we had the start of a nice new friendship. I got up to walk Leslie out to her car while Tommy ordered us a couple of grinders.

It was a clear night, a little chilly, but no wind. Her car was parked right in front of the Stayawhile. She grabbed my hand again, saying, "Come on, let's go inside your car. It's probably warmer and I want to talk to you."

We got inside the Wagoneer and I immediately started it up so I could put on the heat. I turned to Leslie, "So what is it you want to talk about?"

She dropped her head, kind of hiding her face. "You know, it's been a year and a half since I walked out of my relationship."

I hoped whatever she was going to say wouldn't hurt too much. I had just lost my wife and home to a soy bean muncher. I didn't want her to start lecturing me about Linda the Receptionist, or anything like that. With her head still bowed she continued, "In that year and a half time span, I haven't been with another man."

I wondered to myself how that could be possible, but from her next statement I knew it was, "I feel like a goddam virgin all over again."

She was certainly being honest, and in a way it seemed to make her vulnerable. I reached over to put my arm around her. She raised her head, looking at me, "You are going to break my heart, aren't you?" She moved closer, placing her arms around my neck.

I replied, "That, or you are going to break mine."

She pulled me to her. Leslie was an incredibly husky and strong lady. She kissed me with a passion that only a woman who had not allowed herself this pleasure for such a long time could. Her hands and arms moved all over my body, exploring old territory anew. She allowed me the same joy as one of my hands made its way to her large breast. As usual Hoppy rose to the occasion just about the same time that one of Leslie's hands made its way down to greet it. That was all it took. Hoppy began sending message after message: Tell her we love her, tell her never to let us go, yes, stick your tongue in her mouth, what a wonderful woman. . . .

ELEVEN

The demure wife of the ballplayer led Gene Smith out to the Trumbull-Bridgeport quarry area, near to where the motorcycle was hidden. The sportswriter attempted to loosen her up a little, "What is the matter, Mrs. X. Don't you trust me? I assure you, I am not one of those types of men who are the subject of our meeting tonight."

The actor couldn't resist the challenge. Not only did he pattern his outer persona after Ava Gardner, now he was going to try to speak like her. While the "co-star" continued to drive, his thoughts were of his childhood hero, Konstantin Stanislavski, and his Stanislavski Method of acting. Yes, the emotional truth, the inner motivation. There was absolutely nothing like it. The actor speaking with the worldly voice of the up-until-now inimitable Ava Gardner, said, "I'm sure you are not one of that type, Mr. Smith. I am quite positive you will represent this story in your usual style. My immediate concern now is to sit in a nice quiet spot with you and recount the events of the past six months. Turn right at the next corner, please."

The columnist turned down a country road, leaving the streetlights behind. He wasn't sure if it was the scotch, the classy broad sitting beside him, or a combination of all related events, but once the right turn had been made—it was as if he had been transported into a different situation. One beyond his steadfast journalistic way of approaching things. He drove with both hands gripping the steering wheel, transfixed as if this woman beside him had stuck her hand up his anus and was manipulating him as a puppeteer might.

The actor-turned-actress sensed the stiffness in her co-star. "Mr. Smith, please bear with me. I realize that this is extremely unusual. But I assure you, once you understand why I had to go to considerable lengths for privacy, it will all become clear to you."

She opened her purse, reaching for the Evening Enchantment, dabbing a touch on both of her lobes. When she dropped the small bottle of perfume back inside her purse, she conveniently didn't snap the purse shut.

The fragrance, along with her words, seeped into the sportswriter. There was no more feeling of transfixation, now it was a cold sweat. But more disturbing to the columnist was the growing organ between his legs.

The one who pretended to be Ava Gardner now sensed her supremacy and began to confide in her very own sportswriter. "You have no idea what it's been like for me this past half year. How could one feel so unwanted? How terrible it was to find out my husband was seducing young boys." Her voice began to break slightly as the first teardrop emerged. When she spoke again it was with control, but the hurt in the woman was obvious. "Mr. Smith, you just don't know what I've been through." She placed her gloved hand gently on the hand of the driver, saying, "Please help me? Please help me make this go away?"

The sportswriter pulled her hand away from the steering wheel, guiding it to the empty portion of the seat between them. He wished he knew her name, he wished he could pull the car over to the side of the road so he could hold her and allow her to cry it out. Instead, he just held her hand, saying nothing, only breathing a little heavier than normal.

This time when she spoke it was with the same controlled soft

THE FOURTH ESTATE MURDERS

voice, "It's coming up here on the left, just before the large tree. Yes, that's it, turn down there."

He obeyed, driving his car down the dirt road. . . .

Micky and Dave stayed far behind because there were no other cars on the country road. When they watched their pal, Geno, take a right, Dave said, "Hurry, before we lose them."

But when they finally got to the turn, they saw it was just a deserted dirt road. The Mick asked, "What shall we do, Davy?"

"Pull over and shut the lights off."

"I don't like this, Davy. Let's get the hell out of here."

"Keep cool, Micky. We've got to find out what's going on. Turn over there behind those trees. Just in case they come back out, they won't see our car."

Micky seemed worried, asking, "And then what are we going to do?"

Dave tried to ease his tension, "We are newspaper reporters, right?   Well, then, let's go find something to report."

As they were getting out of the car Micky said, "I'm not a goddam newspaper reporter, I'm a sportswriter. . . ."

Leslie left to go and see her sick mother in Hartford. I begged her to stay with me, but she insisted she had to go. She talked to me like a mother might a child, calming me down and saying, "When one has to wait for something, it always makes it better." Just like that she became my girlfriend. Here I was thirty-nine years old, and I finally got myself a girlfriend. She was no spring chicken herself but, my God, the thought of her made me feel like a lovesick kid.

When I reentered the Stayawhile, Tommy was just finishing his grinder. Georgie yelled from behind the bar, "Hey, Jimmy, what take you so long, you give it to her in dee car?"

Tommy sneered, "Sit down and don't pay any attention to that crazy Greek. We're going to have a few drinks tonight." Then he yelled to Georgie, "Bring us some of that Irish whiskey you got hidden, me and my pal here are going to toast his new girl-friend."

"How do you know she's my girlfriend?"

"Because, old buddy, you got gaga eyes. Hey, Georgie, doesn't Jimmy have gaga eyes?"

"Yeah, you eyes gaga."

A couple of Irish whiskeys with Tommy and Georgie and not only were my eyes gaga, but so was my whole body. I ate the grinder Tommy had ordered for me. He seemed to be watching over me, making sure I had enough to eat. Then he asked, "How are your little girls?"

"Ah, they're swell. Not just because they're my daughters, but aren't they great kids?"

He shook his head in agreement, "I love 'em, I love 'em both."

Tommy was in such a good mood, I thought I might tell him about my recurring dream. "Do you remember when that song by Wilson Phillips that came on your car radio this afternoon?"

"You mean the group my girls listen to."

"Yes, them. You see, I've been having this dream that I'm in bed with them. We are doing all sorts of things together."

Tommy's face grew redder than normal. "You are talking about three freakin' kids, you pervert. Have you gone loony in the goddam head, or what?"

"No, no, you've got it all wrong."

"Bullshit, I do. This is probably psychological. You no doubt miss your daughters quite a bit. That Hoppy you always refer to has turned you into a freakin' pervert."

I knew he'd keep harping on this so I accidentally elbowed my beer so it fell his way. He jumped up, but couldn't avoid the

THE FOURTH ESTATE MURDERS

spilling beer in time. "You shithead, you did that on purpose."

I loved getting him upset. I laughed, "No, I didn't. Honest, it was an accident."

"Oh, yeah, how's this for an accident?" He poured his half-full bottle of beer on my head. We both got up and started pushing each other just like old times.

Georgie yelled from behind the bar, "You guys two crazy fucks!"

I yelled back, "No way, Georgie, I'm the crazy one. Tommy here isn't so crazy."

Tommy countered by slapping himself on the face, and asking, "Who's crazy?"

I looked toward the bar, "Georgie, hand me that bottle of Irish whiskey, will you?"

I took down a mammoth gulp and handed the bottle to Tommy. I walked over to old Grumpy Charlie sitting at the end of the bar. I picked up his glass of beer and dumped it on the bar. By this time all the old-timers had begun to watch. Seeing old Charlie all upset elated them, and I received an appreciative round of applause.

Tommy swallowed a great amount of the potent liquor. He had this sly, mischievous way of looking out of the corners of his eyes. He gave me one of those looks and then leaped up onto the bar and took a dive right through all the bottles and glasses that rested on it, knocking down and breaking many in his path.

Georgie yammered! "I one crazy motherfucker, too!" He looked up at the television picked up an empty beer bottle, saying, "I sick of that stupid television and that stupid war! I making this fucking war over now!" He threw the bottle right through the picture tube, which brought applause from everyone, plus the added reward of a pull on the Irish whiskey.

Now it was my turn again. I looked around for anything to

damage. There, in his uniform, sat Scotty with is mailbag dangling off his bar stool. He looked my way; immediate fear came to his eyes. "No, laddie, you'll go to jail for twenty years. This is government property."

I ignored him, pulling out Hoppy and aiming it at the inside of the mailbag. Scotty yelled, "I'll be damned in hell for this! I'm sure of that." He unzippered his own fly and relieved himself all over the inside of the government property.

Georgie bellowed, "The fucking, goddam war over! No more war in this Stayawhile! Tommy, you no let Jimmy be crazier than you."

Tommy looked around in a frenzy. He couldn't think of anything. Everyone kind of settled back onto their stools, giving him the floor. His face was so red it looked like a tomato. Then all of a sudden a serene look came over it. He walked over and grabbed a chair from a table toward the back of the bar and dragged it out to the middle of the floor. He had that sly smile on his face and said, "Hey, Jimmy, do you remember when Leslie said to speak favorably of her this evening. Well, Leslie, I want you to know that I'm glad you let me and my buddy here off the hook. He's lucky that a classy woman like yourself would even give him the time of day. So it's nice to know you."

Tommy picked up the chair. It must have been at least twenty-five years old—who knows, maybe it was fifty. He raised it high over himself, then with his full strength he brought the chair down onto his head, the seat part making contact first. We watched in awe as part of the seat broke away and went flying, while other parts shattered. Tommy had broken a chair over his head. The outer frame of the chair hung on his shoulders while his head stuck out of the middle. We stood quietly waiting for some kind of response from Tommy. He seemed to be in a world of his own. Then, as if he had just received a blessing from heaven itself, he moved closer to me, still wearing part of the chair around his neck, and asked, "Now, whose crazier?"

What could I say? "You are. You win. *You're* crazier, Tommy."

TWELVE

The dirt road came to an end. Ahead, all Gene Smith's headlights revealed was a grassy little tire path. He muttered, "I don't think we can go any further."

The actor playing the role of Ava Gardner still held the sportswriter's hand between them on the car seat. Now she released it and pointed ahead, "Yes. Just on the other side of that old refrigerator, there is a clearing."

Gene Smith drove across the grassy path and on to the other side past the old, discarded refrigerator and out into an open clearing. The actor whispered sensuously, "You can stop here and shut your lights off."

Gene Smith had long ago lost the erection he'd had. The only sensation he felt now was just the slightest twinge of fear. He glanced at the intriguing passenger sitting next to him. She returned his look, allowing him to see the glitter of her wet eyes. The columnist thought it wise to start off slowly, "Would you care for a cigarette?"

She smiled in the darkness, "No, thank you, I don't smoke. I know you came for a story. Just give me a moment more, please?"

The sportswriter sat back, now much more comfortable with the situation. He took a drag on his cigarette, "Are you sure you are comfortable way out here? Wouldn't you prefer to go back to Bridgeport and maybe find a quiet cocktail lounge?"

She wasted no time replying, "Oh, I don't know. I've been so

THE FOURTH ESTATE MURDERS

confused these past few days. It's such a nice evening, can we go outside for a little fresh air?"

The columnist put his cigarette out in the ashtray. "Good idea. Of course we can."

Shortly after they were both outside, she walked toward the old refrigerator, with Gene Smith following close behind. She still managed to stay at least one step ahead of him. "You know, I read that masterful article you did on Victor Kiam and Lisa Olsen. That's how I want you to treat my husband, just like Victor Kiam—show him no mercy."

She slowly reached inside her purse as they moved closer to the old refrigerator.

Gene Smith thought about the Victor Kiam article and wondered what it was that she really liked about it. He thought, She is a woman and no doubt automatically sides with Lisa Olsen, not realizing that neither men nor women actually has anything to do with the column. It was journalism that he was protecting. But because Olsen just happened to be a woman, that made it all the more easy to strike out in the defense of journalists. He responded, "Oh, I didn't really come down that hard on Victor. I just don't like his tactics."

He looked up just in time to see her turn toward him. Pulling her hand out of the purse, she instantly began spraying mace directly onto the sportswriter's face. With her other hand, she reached into the old refrigerator, pulling out a heavy piece of rusty metal. She began her swing, accompanying it with the disguised voice of Victor Kiam's 'Uncle Calvin'. . . "My nephew's a good boy, take back what you said about him!"

The heavy metal struck the maced and bewildered Gene Smith full force on the side of his head. He fell on his back while the murderer watched his whole body shake. The rusty old piece of metal had a dull point at one end. Paul Nelson raised it high in the air over the convulsing body of Gene Smith. Then in a quiet subdued voice, the same one used by the impostor Gene Smith, said. . . . "Remember, Mr. Smith, don't tell anyone that I'm involved."

All of them, Ava Gardner, Uncle Calvin, the impostor Gene Smith and Paul Nelson drove the heavy metal weapon into the chest of the sportswriter.

Paul Nelson waited until he was sure Gene Smith was lifeless. There was no need to go back to the car. He was certain he'd left no evidence of his true identity. He picked up his purse and pulled out his little calling card. He unfolded it, holding it up to the dim moonlight for a final reading:

> *I warned, I warned all those who scorn,*
> *Leaving the reader much forlorn.*
> *Attention you members of the Fourth Estate,*
> *This one's paltering of Kiam sealed his fate.*

He folded the message and put it inside the pants pocket of the very-expired Gene Smith. He had wanted to place it inside the sportswriter's jacket pocket, but there was so much blood coming from the head and chest that he thought the message might get ruined. He began his long walk back up the dirt road to his motorcycle hidden near the main street. . . .

Dave and Micky were just about halfway down the dirt road. Micky asked, "Davy, what if Geno is fucking this broad in his car and he sees us sneaking up on him? What if he's got a gun and he blows our fucking heads off?"

"Micky, cool out. I tell you, there is a story down the road."

Micky McManis gave a whispered chuckle and pointed, "There's more than a story down the road. Look!"

THE FOURTH ESTATE MURDERS

Coming from the other way they could see the silhouette of a woman. "Jesus Christ, Mick! What the hell is going on?"

Paul Nelson had taken his heels off and was holding them in his hands, walking on the dirt road in his stocking feet so he could make better time. He saw the two men approaching. At first he thought of running, then decided to confront them, thinking that they may have followed him and Gene Smith. He opened his blouse and reached under his armpit where he had a knife with a cloth-wrapped handle secured inside the strap of his brassiere. He pulled it out and quickly slipped it into his purse.

The two men were getting closer. With the heels being held by a gloved hand and no doubt his wig and makeup in a mess, he thought it wise not to be Ava Gardner any longer. Instead he assumed the outward manner of a lady who is a bit intoxicated. He unbuttoned the top two buttons of his blouse and wobbled toward the two men.

The three stopped a few paces from one another. Dave Feldman spoke first, "Excuse me, miss, are you by any chance with a gentleman named Gene Smith?"

The trampy-looking woman replied, "I was with him, ahem, but I believe the old boy passed out. Are you his friends?"

The two men exchanged looks. Dave Feldman saw no reason to lie at this point. But he put his snoopy, reporter's nose to work. "Yes, we are his friends. We were worried about him. The three of us had been drinking at one of our favorite bars, then our friend Gene just up and left. He seemed a bit drunk and mentioned that he was going on an interview a little later. So when he left, we followed. Partially for his safety, but more specifically because this fine gentleman and myself are also journalists."

'Reportersss, more reportersss!'

Dave Feldman continued, "He led us to believe he was onto a big story so my colleague here Mr. Michael McManis, and I thought we might try to find out what is going on."

Dave eyed the woman who seemed to be enjoying his short speech. He reached inside his jacket and pulled out his cigarettes. He offered one to the slutty-looking broad; she took it. He put one in his own mouth and then lit them both. Now feeling more sure of himself, he continued, "Might you know something for the record?"

She pushed some of the dangling hairs away from her forehead, careful not to disturb the wig. Then she exhaled some of the cigarette smoke out into the cold, still night. "Well, doll, I might know something about this infamous scoop that brought you two good-looking guys from the big city to way out here in this spooky woods. Yes, I just might know something."

Micky still felt uncomfortable, "Well, ma'am, what's going on?"

'They are all ssso nossey . . . thisss fraternity.'

She blew more smoke out, "Why don't we go and wake up your friend. Then the four of us can find the truth together."

Dave didn't give Micky a chance to answer, "Alright, let's go." Dave Feldman immediately started walking down the dirt road, while the floozy and Micky followed.

The Mick was a little shy around women—especially those who looked sexy. He turned toward this one to try and get better acquainted. In a flash the knife was out of the purse. Paul Nelson never gave Micky a chance to speak. He plunged the knife into the Adam's apple of Micky McManis. Dave, hearing the gasp, turned, only to be met by a heavy spray of mace. Before the reporter could react to this, Paul Nelson drove his blade deep into the gut of Dave Feldman. Then pulling out the knife, he slit both their jugulars. The whole action took no more than a minute.

It had all become clear to Paul Nelson—the reason he didn't trust members of the Fourth Estate. It didn't matter to them what they wrote about other people—or other countries for that matter, they just wanted to sell news at the cost of anyone or anything. That is, as long as it didn't include themselves. They hardly ever examined their own mistakes and they practically never criticized one another individually. That's what he despised, "The Fraternity of the Fourth Estate".

Since he hadn't known he was going to meet these two, he had not composed a message. He could not bring himself to exit this stage without leaving some type of calling card—something that would further warn the press. And yes, something that would include the dramatics of the evening. He reached inside the jacket pocket of poor Micky McManis, and took out a pen and a piece of paper. *'Yesss, dearesst William, . . . Hamlet! O good Horatio!'*

> *Of carnal, bloody, and unnatural acts;*
> *Of accidental judgements, casual slaughters;*
> *Of deaths put on by cunning, and forc'd cause;*
> *And in this upshot, purposes mistook*
> *Fall'n on the inventor's heads:*
> *All this can I truly deliver.*

He carefully folded the piece of paper and put it and the pen back into Micky's jacket pocket. It was a fine performance from start to finish. He had learned so much from the dirty world of journalism. He knew he couldn't go on forever killing members of the press. It was over. These murders would cause many questions to be answered. He knew none would ever admit it, but he was certain that a more responsible approach to journalism would now take hold. He was all done. He would disappear. They would never find out who killed all these members of the press. That, in itself would keep them on their toes.

He took both Dave's and Micky's wallets and jewelry, as he

had always done with his victims. After all, he had to eat. Identification cards were invaluable for forged future identities. He would go back to the St. Clair Boarding House, gather up his few belongings, then return to the Oak Tree Trailer Park. From there he would depart the following night. Only then, in the darkness of the night, would he be able to slip out from under those watchful eyes of the repulsive Blanche Herman.

He knew where he was going, he had planned it. It would be near a theater; he always needed to be close to a playhouse. But before he could leave, it was necessary for him to inform his previously selected audient of his latest presentation. . . .

The phone's ring sounded like a tiny jackhammer inside my head. I attempted to rise, twice falling back on the bed. But the ringing persisted. I tried to get myself together, pulling my tongue off the roof of my mouth and parting my lips that were stuck together. I wondered what time it was while I slowly fumbled for the phone, finally grabbing hold of it. "Yeah, yeah. Hello, already."

"Hey, shit-for-brains. Sleepin', huh? C'mon, man, better wake up. I got a surprise for ye."

I shook my aching head, "Harland! Jesus Christ, it's you."

"Hey, man, don't use the Lord's name in vain."

"You evil bastard! You're sick! Turn yourself in before you hurt someone else."

"That's what the fuck I'm tryin' to tell ye, man. U'm afraid I already have."

I pulled myself up and leaned against the headboard. "Why are you telling me this?"

"Because, man, ye said ye was a sports fan. Right? Well, sport, here's a mother-fuckin' sports flash for ye. Take a ride up to the Trumbull-Bridgeport quarry. Drive down Old Country Road until

THE FOURTH ESTATE MURDERS

ye see a white Ford parked on the side of the road. Hang a left down that dirt road. Ye'll be seein' some sports before ye go all the way to the end, but don't forget to keep goin'. Later." He hung up.

I called Tommy. He sounded as bad as I felt. I told him about Harland's call and said I'd be over his house to pick him up in twenty minutes. I stuck my head under the faucet allowing the cold water to counteract the effects of the Irish whiskey. I dressed and left.

Tommy was already waiting for me outside his house, probably because he didn't want to wake up any of his kids. He had his uniform on, I guessed he wasn't planning to return home but instead going straight to work when he was finished. Before he had even gotten inside the car he started talking, "What the hell did we do to ourselves last night?" Not allowing me to answer, he continued, "Did you bring your Beretta?"

"Yes, I've got it. Do you think there might be any trouble?"

"Always be ready, Jimmy. You should know that by now."

"My head, Tommy. My head is killing me."

"I know. Don't talk about it. Why the hell did this Harland start calling you anyway?"

"It's just a disguise, Tommy. There's no such person as Harland."

"Are you sure? I don't want us to go into the quarry and find ourselves up against fifty bikers or anything like that."

"Yes, I'm sure. All the people we're looking for are the same person. The Puerto Rican, Robin Harris, the cowboy, Harland and who knows who else? What I don't understand is how one individual could do all this and still keep tabs on the person whose tracking him?"

Tommy thought for a moment and then offered, "Maybe he put a bug in your office just like he did at the Barnes'."

"But why?"

"Possibly he heard a conversation on the Barnes' bug about them deciding to hire you."

"Yes, it would be a smart move. Certainly true to this murderer's M.O. He never makes mistakes."

The sun was just starting to rise, Tommy looked over at me, "Listen, Jimmy. Everybody makes mistakes. Sometimes the solution to the problem is finding out when and where the mistake was made."

We drove down Old Country Road as the night made its subtle change to day. Tommy pointed to the white Ford. I slowly took the left down the dirt road that Harland had described. The Wagoneer crept along, seemingly acting as careful as we were.

There they were—two dead bodies laid out in the glistening morning dew. My heart began to pound as I followed Tommy out to the two victims. We were both careful not to disturb anything while we examined them. Neither had a wallet nor jewelry. But the one who had been stabbed in the neck had a note in his inside-jacket pocket. We read it, then put it back the way we had found it, not wishing to hide any further evidence from the police—not like the Walblont note.

Shortly thereafter, we continued down the dirt road to the other parked car. There we found another bloodied victim also relieved of his belongings, but with yet another note. I smelled a familiar scent of perfume, but couldn't place it. After we'd read the note, we got out of there as quickly as possible. We didn't speak to one another while we were driving to Tommy's car. When we were almost there, Tommy said, "I'll inform the police. Believe me they won't know who the tip came from. Where are you going after you drop me off?"

I was just beginning to breath normally again. "I'm going to find out if there's a bug planted in my office. How about you, are you going to work now?"

"No, it's still too early. I'm thinking about taking a ride out to Southport just to see if that Nelson guy came back yet."

"Do you want me to go with you?"

"No, go check out your office. But listen, Jim, just don't leave until you hear from me. Alright?"

I nodded in agreement. Tommy knew how I felt about killing. I just didn't have the stomach for it. He placed his hand on my shoulder, saying, "Don't worry, Jimmy, we'll get this bastard. You be careful, just remember who's the crazy one here." He gave me that sly smile of his and got out.

When I returned to the office, I searched everywhere. First the bedroom, then the bathroom. Nothing. I tried all the pictures hanging on the walls. Then my desk—over it, through it and underneath it—all along the floorboards, and inside the electrical fixtures. Then all of a sudden I felt it before I even saw it. It was pushed into one of the seams of my couch, right near the desk. The microphone was completely exposed. I yanked it out, not knowing what to do with it next, so I destroyed it.

I wanted to get out of the office. I needed to do something, but I had told Tommy I'd wait here for him. What I should have done was to have gone with him.

The ache in my head from the previous evening was a constant reminder of how foolish Tommy and I could really be. All of our lives, in one way or another, we would showboat. I would think about the lives of most other men. They seemed so settled, like they took a certain path and followed that direction, no matter where it took them. Not us, we were still middle-aged kids, somewhat uncertain about what we were going to do when we grew up.

The phone rang. It was too soon to be Tommy, so I hoped it wouldn't be Harland again with another wicked message. Instead it was Leslie. She was back from Hartford and at her apartment. She told me briefly that her mother was fine. Then I told her about my call and what Tommy and I had done this morning. She said she had a few hours before she had to be at work and wanted to stop by the office. I told her it would be fine and to bring something for my aching head. . . .

It was extremely foggy. Southport, being right on Long Island Sound, experiences dense fog quite often; especially after a cold spell abruptly changes to damp, warm weather. The Oak Tree Trailer Park was right off of Route 1, which was now very busy with morning commuter traffic. Tommy Harrington parked his station wagon on the street just in case this Nelson fellow was home. And if he wasn't, then he wouldn't disturb anyone else's morning. Blanche Herman might get suspicious seeing him or Jimmy there everyday looking for her wonderful Mr. Nelson.

He walked directly to the Air Stream trailer that Mrs. Herman had pointed out to be Nelson's. The fog was a perfect cover. It was so thick between the trailers that no one would be able to see him with his police uniform on. He moved closer to the Air Stream, quite easily observing that there was no car parked in that trailer's designated spot. He thought of knocking on the door, but because he was almost certain there was no one there, he decided, instead, to try peeking through a few windows. The front of the trailer overlooked the rest of the park while the back was flush with the woods. He walked around to the woods side to further conceal his presence. There was a large clearing around back, away from the trailer. It had stacks of firewood and a few wheelbarrows; a car and a motorcycle were parked there, too. The car looked like it hadn't been used for quite some time. There were dead leaves and bird droppings all over it. He realized he was completely hidden from view. He wouldn't be seen as long as no one needed any firewood.

The trailer rocked a little as he pulled himself up for a look inside. To his dismay, it was too dark to see anything, but he noticed that the window wasn't entirely shut. So using his palm, he pushed it upwards without any problem—the window opened wide. He thought it best not to waste any time. With a quick surge of energy, he boosted himself up and halfway through the window. He couldn't help but think how this would impress his good friend. Jimmy always bragged about doing things like this to get information. That was his thing, to do and go places where police couldn't. He claimed that was how he got results.

Getting the rest of the way inside was a little more difficult than Tommy had anticipated. He had to hold on with one hand while he reached down and undid his pistol-laden belt with the other hand. He dropped both items onto the trailer's inside floor, and soon found himself belly-down next to them.

When he picked himself up, Tommy found he was in a dark maze of clothes. The obscure, fogged light coming in from the lone window showed him enough to realize that the entire room was packed full of clothes—hanging and in open crates. There were also numerous boxes of stage costumes. He knew this was only a small room in a small trailer, yet he felt he was lost. He began frantically pushing clothes aside, creating a passageway through the maze to a wall, any wall. When he finally reached one, he made sure he kept one hand on the wall at all times. He moved along, inching around stacked boxes, blindly, until he finally felt a door, then a doorknob.

To Tommy's pleasure, there was light when he opened the door. As he peered around, he saw that the rest of the trailer was uncluttered. All he could think about was getting out, but not through the same window. He started walking toward the door. All the moving around he had done seemed to re-ignite his hangover. He walked by the bathroom and for the briefest of moments he thought he saw an ethereal figure. Instinct told him to head quickly for the exit. He reached for his revolver. Too late! In the next instant something course was thrown over his head. His keen sense of smell told him it was burlap. Blindly he turned to confront his attacker. At just that moment he felt the cold steel enter his body just below the abdomen! Before the blade completed its penetration, Tommy heard a sound similar to that of the opening of a vacuumed-packed can of coffee. Then came an odor, not unlike that of the Stayawhile Tavern. The pain was horrifying as Tommy withered to the floor. . . .

Leslie was at my office in twenty minutes. When I opened the door, it was like we hadn't seen each other for days. We threw ourselves at one another in a loving embrace. I would have just as soon stayed cradled in her arms the whole day, but she pushed me away, talking to me again as if I were a child. She kidded, "What happened to my little Raindrop? Did he hurt his little heady playing? Mommy brought Raindrop some aspirin for his boo-boo."

Despite what I had told Leslie about the murders, she seemed a little amused by my condition. I grabbed the bottle. "Thanks, Leslie, and don't call me Raindrop."

She studied me as I swallowed down a few aspirins with some water. She could see I was pretty upset. She ordered, "Come over here on the couch and put your head on my lap." I did as she said. She stroked my forehead, not unlike the way my mother used to do.

In no time she had eased the ache in my head. Even though she was very feminine, she was also incredibly brawny. I thought of Sally, who had found romance and companionship with the lean, tofu-eating Blake Lennon. Even so, I couldn't help but be happy for her, but I was more happy for myself. It was a love-hate thing I had with women I thought were more intelligent than myself. I hardly ever went out of my way to make friends with them, but whenever I did, at the very least there was always respect and admiration. And only once before I had been able to find love—that was with Sally. Now, here it was coming again, growing like a trailing rose, with no way to control it. Even trying to cut it made it grow stronger.

While I lay on her lap, I reached up to pull her to me, but she repulsed the gesture. "No, not now. I have to go to work in a while."

"Then, when?"

She shrugged her shoulders, "I guess when we both want to." Then she broadened her smile, "But soon, I think."

She urged me to tell her most of what Tommy and I were involved in. Leslie listened intently to all I had to say, at times looking horrified at the thought of this killer among us. She was of the opinion that it was too dangerous for Tommy and me to handle alone, especially now that the killer was phoning me. Even worse, that he had bugged my office. She wondered aloud how I could do such gruesome work. Then I reminded her that she wrote obituaries. After I had said it, I couldn't help but think what a waste of talent it was having this lady, this fine artist, do such a loathsome job.

Shortly thereafter, she was gone. She urged me to be careful and to call her periodically during the day. I gladly agreed to do so. It was becoming all too good to be true. A woman besides Sally who cared about what I did. These days, for most of the time it was Tommy who looked after me. . . .

Blanche Herman was delighted when she saw who it was at the door. "Mr. Nelson, you're back! Oh, how nice." She smiled as she opened the door to allow her visitor to enter.

Paul Nelson had gone so far away from himself he scarcely knew how to stop acting. Just like a liar who has told too many lies—truth and falsehoods become indistinguishable. He would be Paul Nelson for this one last act and then nevermore. "Hello, Blanche. So sorry to barge in on you without warning."

"Not at all, Paul. You must know by now how I feel about you. Won't you sit down? Can I make you some breakfast?"

"Not at this time, thank you, I'm in an awful hurry."

She sensed the slightest strain in his voice. "Is there something wrong?"

He could see she was already showing signs of sympathy for him. "Yes, Blanche, there is. Has anyone been here looking for me?"

She thought for a moment then answered, "Only two very nice friends of my brother-in-law, Louis. They were looking to employ your acquaintance, Robin Harris. This was only yesterday. Why? Is there something I should know about them?"

"No, no, don't give it a second thought. I was expecting a call from an I.R.S. representative. Taxes, you know. I'm afraid I filed late last year."

She thought, He is such an honest man. If only she could think of some way to impress him, maybe he would show a little more emotion toward her. She said, "Then you won't mind if I call up Louis' friends up. They would like to get in touch with Mr. Harris."

He began to move toward the door. "Please do, Blanche. That's so very nice of you."

He started to open the door, then turned to her. "Oh! Would you, by any chance, be able to cash a check for me? The banks aren't open yet and I do need some money."

She always had cash available. Most of the transient campers who stopped for a night or a week usually paid in cash. She was more than happy to accommodate Paul Nelson. "That shouldn't be a problem. How much do you want?"

"Is three hundred okay?"

She nodded, assuring him, "I have more if you'd like it?"

"No, that will be fine."

He watched her walk down the trailer's tiny hallway to her bedroom. She opened her bottom dresser drawer where she kept her cash box and jewelry. Politely she called out, "Are all fifties okay?"

He knew that the moment had come and there was no time for questions or a drawn out performance. '*That bourgeois detective isss closse.*'

She was still on her knees, counting the fifties one more time, when she felt the palm of his hand on her face. For a flash she perceived it as a sexual caress, then swiftly came the sharp blade swiping across her neck to the juggler. . . .

Tommy was being bounced around in the room full of clothes as the trailer started moving. His hands and feet were bound, so it was impossible to do anything about the knife wound in his gut. He had heard about knifings in that location. They occurred all the time in the Puerto Rican barrios. Just below the abdomen—you would hardly kill anyone knifing them there, just cause them tremendous pain.

He felt as if he was bleeding inside as his mind tried to fathom where this crazy bastard was taking him. He wondered if Jimmy was getting worried about him. He thought that Jimmy would somehow be his only hope. But the pain kept on coming. His little girls, he would have to concentrate on his daughters and his sweet wife, Alice. . . .

Where the hell was Tommy? Why hadn't he called yet? That stupid, roly-poly mick! He was going to hear about this from me! I'd never allow him to forget this one. Big time cop—yeah, sure. I knew all along I should never have taken on this stupid case. Money, goddam money, that's what did it! Who the hell did the Barnses think they were? Did they think they could just buy anyone? If there's a crazy person out there who wants to kill people—well, that's not my problem. Please, God, let Tommy call and I'll drop this case. I won't whore around any-more—TOMMY, PICK UP THE GODDAMN PHONE!!!

Twice I called up the Bridgeport Police but Tommy still hadn't shown up for work. There was the possibility he was having car trouble, like a flat tire. He always rode around on bald tires. A cop with five kids who wasn't on the take just couldn't afford new tires.

Finally the damn phone rang. "Where the hell have you been?"

Leslie's voice replied, "Jimmy, what is wrong? I'm at work."

"Oh, Leslie, I'm still waiting for Tommy. He hasn't called me yet. I'll go out of my mind if he doesn't call me soon."

She hesitated for a moment, then said sternly, "Calm down, Jimmy. Losing control won't help anything."

I took a deep breath, "Yes, I know, you're right. I'm just worried."

"I know you are. I don't think Tommy would want you to panic."

"Of course not, but I can't stand just waiting here. I'm thinking of putting the answering machine on then taking a ride out to Southport."

"Wait, I'll come over there and answer your phone while you are gone."

"Oh, Leslie, please hurry."

"I'll leave in five minutes. By the way, the police have found

THE FOURTH ESTATE MURDERS

the bodies of the three dead men. They were all sportswriters."

After we hung up, I paced the floor—back and forth—thinking of all the people I could blame for getting Tommy and me involved in this. Deep down, I knew the blame was ours, but I couldn't face that, at least not now.

The phone rang again. I grabbed it, looking up to heaven and asking to let it be Tommy. "Hello."

"Hey, shit-for-brains! How did ye like my trifecta of sportswriters? Nice job, huh?"

"You son-of-a-bitch! You're sick, goddam sick!"

"Yeah, man, tell me about it. How 'bout ye, garlic breath? Jimmy Conte something special, er what?"

"Jesus Christ, Harland, you're mad."

"Hey, man, I already told ye twice, don't use the Lord's name in vain."

"What do you mean? Who the hell are you kidding? You might be the only living thing Jesus Christ couldn't love."

He laughed, "Yeah, man, you're right, but listen, let's cut the shit. I got your dickhead, cop friend."

"Oh, no! Harland, please listen, don't hurt him."

"Hell, I already stuck a blade in his guts. The fuckin' guy smells, man. What the hell does he eat—dog shit?"

I had to pull myself together. "Harland, is Tommy alive?"

"Yeah, man, he's alive. Why the fuck ye think I called?"

"What do you want?"

"Money, garlic breath, right now. How much ye got?"

"You mean, here, on me?"

"Yeah, ye stupid fuck. By now it must be apparent I bugged your office. I know that dip-shit Barnes has given ye some serious cash. Say the magic number and ye get dickhead back. Don't and then I slit his fag-mick throat."

"Wait, Harland! Don't hang up. Let me go and count what I

have."

Fortunately I had plenty of money because I had cashed seven thousand dollars of what Mr. Barnes had given me so far. Unfortunately I'd paid loads of bills plus I gave Tommy over a thousand. I gathered every cent in the office and went back to the phone. "Harland, I have around twenty five hundred dollars."

There was a brief pause, then, "Bingo, ding-ding-ding. Ye fucking win, ass-wipe. Ye win back the smelly-assed, dick-head."

Stay calm, I kept saying to myself, stay calm. "Harland I want to speak to Tommy? Is he there?"

"Yeah, shit-face, he's here. What the fuck ye think I am, a welcher?"

"Let me speak to him?"

"Yeah, I thought ye'd want to. Hang on I gotta stick this phone through the goddam window, then go stand dickhead up inside the trailer."

They were in a trailer. That all made sense. I should have insisted on going with Tommy to Southport. I heard some noise and a groan—then Harland. "Hey, shit-for-brains, are ye ready? Heeeres's dickhead."

"Tommy! Tommy, are you there?"

There was a little strained breathing, then in a voice just above a whisper, he moaned, "Jimmy, is that you?"

"Yes, Tommy, I'm here."

"Jimmy, I'm hurt bad."

"I know, Tom, hang on, I'm coming to get you, don't worry, I'm coming to get you."

I waited for him to say anything. Then finally, "Tell Alice I love her, always."

I had to hurry, he sounded like he was fading, "You tell her, it sounds like she's going to be taking care of you for a while."

I waited and waited, then he spoke again, "You were the best center fielder, Jimmy."

He was rambling, "Come on, Tommy, hang in there, clear up your head. Please, Tom, don't let me down."

He gave me a slight encouraging chuckle, "Sorry I called you a pervert last night."

Then I heard Harland's voice, "Alright, dickhead, that's enough." He was back on the phone, "Satisfied, shit-for-brains?" Harland told me that he was at a phone booth in Danbury, Connecticut. He gave me the directions to get to it. I was supposed to go there and wait for his call. He would tell me where to go from there. He said that calling the police was entirely up to me. If I thought they would help save Tommy's life, I should call. If I didn't, I shouldn't. I knew what he was implying and was totally prepared to take the chance and play it his way.

Leslie was coming in just as I was leaving. I explained to her as quickly as I could what was happening. She looked shocked, then insisted on coming with me. I said no, over and over again while she followed me down the back stairs.

Georgie was out back dumping his garbage cans. I yelled, "Georgie, you still got that shotgun in your kitchen?"

"Yeah, I have, Jimmy. What for you need?"

"Just get it. Now!"

Georgie ran inside the back door of the Stayawhile while Leslie continued to argue, "I'm going with you."

"It's too dangerous, besides I'm supposed to go alone."

"Then I'll follow you in my car."

"No."

Georgie was back out with the shotgun. "There trouble, I go with you."

Crazy Georgie and Leslie were impeding my progress. I conceded, "Alright! You two can go in Leslie's car. Leslie, tell

Georgie what's happening with Tommy. If he decides he wants to get out after he learns what he's up against, you're both out of it, okay?" They both agreed, "From this point on, you two do as I say. Follow me to Danbury. When I'm a block or so away from the phone booth, I'll wave for you to pull over. Stay there until I come back to get you."

Leslie was about to take issue with my instructions, but I was already inside my Wagoneer.

We drove straight up Route 25, then took the back roads to Danbury. I took chances, passing cars on almost-blind curves. Behind me, Leslie was doing the same thing. I had my little Beretta inside my jacket pocket. If the need arose, I hoped I was prepared to use it. I couldn't understand why there were so many crazy people. Everyday there were new atrocities: children killing their parents, parents killing their children, wide-ranging child abuse—it seemed like everybody was getting into it. Not me. I would get this psycho, but I had no intention of killing him. If he forced me to defend myself, I'd shoot him in the leg or something like that. My objective was to outsmart him, not kill him. I really wouldn't care the least single bit if he got away with all the money and his crimes as long as I got Tommy. That was all that mattered. After all, he wasn't after us, he was killing newspaper people. And I figured as long as he was in his Harland costume, which I had seen him in anyway, he could be reasoned with. I supposed he had had plenty of opportunities to kill me and he hadn't. I guess that's why I hardly had any dread of him, but that didn't stop me from being almost crazy with fear for Tommy's safety.

The directions were simple: just before the turn onto Route 7, there were two roadside telephones. I slowed down, sticking my arm out of the window. I signaled for Leslie and Georgie to pull over. Her headlights went on and off a few times, acknowledging my instructions. They pulled off the blacktop and stopped. After another few hundred yards, I pulled my car into the roadside rest area.

The telephones were a few car-lengths apart. Both had long extension wires so you could sit inside your car and talk. I got out and picked up each receiver to make sure they had dial tones. Then I paced, up and down the parking lot, never wandering from within ear-shot of the phones.

It seemed like hours. And, in fact, it was approaching an hour, yet I still hadn't heard from Harland. I worried that I wasn't at the correct parking area. Maybe the whole thing was just a terrible hoax. He had talked so nasty on the phone. It was possible he just enjoyed upsetting people. Then the phone rang, I felt trepidation and relief at the same time. I answered.

"I knew ye could do it. How's it going, shit-for-brains?"

"Come on, Harland, cut the crap! How's Tommy?"

"Oh, dickhead? He's bleedin' man. I'm gonna have to fumigate the trailer, it ain't fit to walk into, dickhead stinks so much."

"Listen to me, Harland. Don't do any further harm to him. If anything else happens, I'll hunt you down if it takes the rest of my life."

"Then what, man? Ye gonna kiss my ass, 'cause we both know that's all yer capable of. Right?"

"Let's just get this thing over with. I have your money. Tell me what you want me to do?"

"Got to cross the state line. Me and dickhead are in New York State. Don't worry, man, it's close. Less than half an hour."

Harland gave me the directions to Brewster, New York and from there to Lake Carmel. Most of the drive would be on Interstate 84. They weren't far from the exit, and I was familiar with the area. I asked him, "What do you want me to do when

I get to this place?"

There was a long pause, then he answered, "Christ, man, ye gonna have to figure that one out yourself." He hung up. . . .

Tommy had been fading in and out. In a way it felt better like this. His weakened state had helped to somewhat diminish the pain. He felt two hands under his armpits and vaguely could hear a friendly voice. "Come on, fella, let's go get some fresh air."

Everything was blurry for Tommy, but he was encouraged by this folksy person who had obviously untied him. He reached deep down for strength and picked himself up with the aid of this new intimate. One step at a time, together they made it to the other side of the trailer.

The sun was way too bright for Tommy, who closed his eyes, putting his arms around the helpful person, letting whoever it was lead the way—away from that terrible trailer. He felt his body against what seemed to be a tree and, with the help of his companion, he sat down with his back resting against it. That familiar, friendly voice, said, "Okay, pal, you just relax. This will only take a moment."

He felt a rope being tied around his chest and under his armpits. Twice, his friend spun the rope around him. . . .

The murderer had already secured the other end of the rope around the rear bumper of his car. He got in and started the engine, putting it in gear and hoisting the uniformed cop up the tree where the first two branches spread out horizontally from the trunk. He was going to do something he had always wanted to do, but had never gotten the opportunity. Actually it was his conversation with Jimmy Conte that reminded him of the idea.

As an artist he had always reveled at the sight of Jesus Christ nailed to the cross. The serene holiness of the spectacle had indeed been awe-inspiring for him. Whether it was a painting or an acting production, there was so much you could do with the subject. Alas, time was short, he would have to make do with the few creative moments he had.

Tommy felt himself hanging freely but occasionally touching the tree with his body. He could hear a vehicle coming toward him, then felt the roof of it under his feet. Moments later he heard someone else on the roof making the sound of feet walking on metal. The person's hands touched his cheeks. It was that folksy voice, "How are you doing, pal? This won't take long. Go with it and you may find yourself resting alongside Mona Lisa."

Tommy felt his hand being opened; he did nothing to object. All of a sudden there was a different person with him. The voice was deep and operatic, "Facilis decensus a verns." *The dessscent to hell iss eassy.*

First there was a pinch, then he felt the nail being driven through his hand and into the tree limb. So much pain; there was so much pain. Then the person began to pry open his other hand, Tommy tried to resist but was much too weak. "Dis aliter visum." *Man propossesss, God disspossesss.*

Again the now dreaded pinch, then the driving of the large nail through the hand and into the other tree limb.

The crucifier ripped the police shirt from Tommy's body, saying, "Dura lex sed lex." *The law iss hard, but it iss the law.*

There was no time to nail the feet to the trunk of the tree. He wrapped a rope around the policeman's chest, then jumped off the car and tied another rope around the tree trunk and Tommy's ankles.

Aah yesss, Longfellow:

Art is long, and Time is fleeting,
And our hearts, though stout and brave,
Still, like muffed drums, are beating

Funeral marches to the grave.

He pulled the car out from under Tommy's feet and out of his own way for a better view of his creation. Satisfied, he intoned, "Dominus vobiscum." *God be with you.*

THIRTEEN

After Harland's call, I drove back to where Leslie and Georgie were waiting. Both had kind of a daunted look on there faces, no doubt just beginning to realize the seriousness of what they had gotten themselves into. I gave them the directions to where we were going, informing them of the sign marked "Skeeter Hill" that Harland had directed me to over the phone. I'd drive in alone. They would have to wait on the main road.

Leslie was holding my hand through the car window while I spoke. Neither she nor Georgie said anything. I figured I didn't have much time, but for their sakes I thought I'd give them one more try. "Listen guys, there's really no reason for you to go any further. Why don't you just wait in a coffee shop here in Danbury, and after I rescue Tommy, we'll meet you there."

Georgie leaned forward so I could see his face from behind Leslie. "No, Jimmy. I go. Come on, now we get Tommy."

Leslie looked me in the eyes, squeezing my hand, "Just be as careful as you can be." She removed her hand from mine and said, "I'm ready. Let's go."

The drive through Danbury was a pain in the neck. We had to go right through the center of the city to get to Route 84. But once we were on the Interstate, we began to move fast again.

Tommy realized he was almost dead. The terrible pain he had experienced earlier was now a fading sensation. He thought it must be death because he kept imaging himself in his first basketball uniform of his C.Y.O. team. They were so proud of themselves—little kids who had won the league championship, which forced the church to buy them uniforms. They had no choice. Their team was going to the playoffs mainly because of Tommy's basketball skills. He had poured in forty points against St. Jude's—a much taller team that was supposed to beat them. But Tommy had led his team to victory and was mobbed by his teammates. Now because of him they had become respectable; they knew this meant the church would have to buy them uniforms. "Three cheers for Tommy. Hip-hip hooray"

Everything looked so murky. He desperately tried to focus on the man who had done this to him. First there was the filmy outline of the trailer, then the opaque image of the man. What was he? Why had he done this? Tommy strained to see him. Yes, he could see him clearly now.

The man stopped what he was doing to return Tommy's stare. He walked up to the crucified figure, offering him a taste of Harland, "Ye think ye know me, dickhead?"

Tommy looked down, clearly seeing who he was, then whispering an unintelligible response. Harland yelled up to him, "What'd ye say, dickhead?"

It was all Tommy could do to get it out. He wanted desperately to upset this traitor to society. He reached deep inside for it. Then it came easily as if some supernatural force had aided him. He whispered. "I forgive you, my son."

Harland stood dumbfounded, trying to blurt out some crude reply, but nary a word would come from his lips. He took a few steps backward, then a few more, then he turned and ran back to the trailer.

He took what he needed from the trailer, stuffing it into his car. He would have to hurry to get the car away from here. But first, the gasoline cans. He doused the whole trailer inside, then outside—even the tires. There was no room for error, the trailer had to be completely destroyed. . . .

Harland's directions were straightforward. Less than an hour after our last telephone conversation, I found myself in a remote mountainous section of Lake Carmel. I stopped in front of an old dilapidated sign that read "Skeeter Hill". I waved for Leslie to pull over, which she did. I figured that instead of going back to them for any mutual support, I had better just continue on as quickly as possible. I took the little Beretta out; it was loaded and ready. I kept reminding myself that, if need be, I'd be able to shoot him in the leg or something like that. The thought of even having to use the pistol brought on a wave of nausea. Georgie had the shotgun with him; I figured they would be safe enough. We were all on our own.

I turned down the lane. The trees were so overgrown I couldn't see the sky. It was obvious that a vehicle had preceded me here, as evidenced by the broken branches. I realized that this killer could easily ambush me from anywhere. On the other hand, I figured he would want to see some cash before he tried anything.

The foliage overhead was beginning to thin out. I noticed smoke rising up ahead with increasing thickness. I stepped on the accelerator. The tree branches crashed hard against the Wagoneer, causing considerable noise and damage. What I was beginning to see more and more clearly was frightening. Then I pulled out into the open field. Just ahead was the trailer, completely afire and engulfed in black smoke.

I didn't know what to do. Panicky, I looked around but saw no one. I grabbed the Beretta from the dashboard and got out of the car. The clearing looked like an old pasture surrounded by woodland. I moved closer to the burning trailer, noticing through all the smoke a lone tree off to one side. I looked, then looked again, trying to discern what was only a vague image. Then as I moved closer, I thought my eyes must be deceiving me—it couldn't be! I ran through a wall of smoke. "Tommy! Tommy! No, no, no!" Oh God, he'd nailed Tommy to the tree. I dropped the Beretta and ran over to him, reaching up to touch his ankle. "Don't worry, Tommy. I'll have you down in no time."

He looked like he was sleeping. He must have passed out. I had to get him down. "Please, Tommy, hold on!"

I could see fresh tire marks next to the tree. That bastard! That's how he had gotten Tommy up there. "Don't worry, buddy, I'm here. Hold on."

I ran back through the smoke to the Wagoneer. I'd get him down the same way that bastard had put him up there. . . .

He looked through the trees at the goings-on by the fire. *'Some detective, Jimmy Conte. You look like you are going to go pee-pee in your pantsss.'*

He would wait a little longer until his prey had become totally engrossed in the task of getting his police friend off the tree.

I hurried back with the Wagoneer, pulling it up underneath Tommy's feet. As I was climbing up onto the Wagoneer's roof, I wondered how I was going to get those appalling nails out of Tommy's hands. "Tommy, what has he done to you." I was now standing directly in front of him. I slowed down. He looked so peaceful, almost childlike. I didn't need to feel for a heartbeat or pulse—he was dead. "If only you could have held on a little longer. I was coming. I would have saved you. You shouldn't have died. You knew I'd be coming. "The tears flowed, "What about Alice and the girls? What are they going to do without you???"

THE FOURTH ESTATE MURDERS

He watched while the fire still roared. He would have to take this detective out soon. Somebody, by now, had probably sighted the smoke and would either come up themselves to investigate, or send in the fire-fighters. Although he had plenty of money on hand, a little more wouldn't hurt. But that wasn't why he needed to kill James Conte. The killer had become afraid of him. The detective seemed to know a little more than everyone else. He had allowed the investigator to come a little too close, even though it had given him an opportunity to perform in a situation the likes of which he had never tried before. It was now time to finish off the lone audient. He slowly began to creep out of the wooded area. With a .45 in his hand, he thought he'd simply fill the private dick with lead, grab the money and be gone. But wait! He had to hold his ground. *'That woman. What isss she doing here? . . .'*

Leslie ran through the billowing smoke screen to where Jimmy was standing on the Wagoneer, talking to Tommy. She could easily see that the absolute worst had happened. She gently called up to him, "Jimmy, why don't you come down. There isn't anything you can do. I'll tell Georgie to go and get the local police. Okay?"

He made no response of any kind, instead he seemed to be locked into a frozen stare.

She climbed up on the Wagoneer to be next to him. Only then did he speak, "If he just could have held on a little longer, I'd have saved him."

Leslie was shaking inside but refused to break down. "I know, Jimmy. Come on now, let's get down from here."

He offered no resistance as she carefully guided him off the roof of the Wagoneer. . . .

'*Sshe will have to die with her lover boy.*'

He thought of the most wonderful artistic things he could do with their bodies. But there was no time for that now. Two quick deaths, that was all there was to it. He scanned the area, making sure there was no one around before he went out to meet Romeo and Juliet. But just before he set foot onto the clearing, Georgie appeared—stomping along, waving a shotgun.

'*It's that idiot from the Ssstayawhile. Hesss too unpredictable. Let them enjoy their grief.*'

He ran off through the woods to where his car was parked on the other side of Skeeter Hill.

FOURTEEN

I was trying to get myself together. I had to dress up for Tommy's funeral. I looked around my bedroom. It was a complete mess. I had broken just about everything in it, besides making numerous holes in the wall with my fists. The last few days had been the worst kind of nightmare imaginable. It started right after Tommy's death, and still hadn't stopped.

On that terrible day, Georgie had returned in a short time with the local police. But before they could take Tommy off the tree, they needed photographs. Soon some newspaper people came along and talked the police into keeping Tommy up there a little longer for their own photographs. Leslie insisted that they take him down, but the police chief claimed that first they needed the county coroner to pronounce him dead.

Then came the T.V. people. They all wanted an interview. Leslie kept everyone away from me, answering all questions herself, lying whenever she had to protect me.

When it was decided that the best way to free Tommy's hands was to pull the nail heads right through them, the media's attention returned to poor Tommy. I watched while they lifted my friend down, then losing sight of him as he was lowered into the crowd that surrounded him. It was awful; the whole scene was horrific.

By the day's end, much of the story had reached the public. "The Fourth Estate Murderer", as they chose to call him, had left a trail of blood throughout southern Connecticut. My name was all over the news. Half of what they reported had never actually happened, but it didn't really matter.

I heard their was a television crew over at Tommy's house trying to get an interview with Alice and asking without permission questions of his daughters. Alice had tried to speak to me on more than one occasion during the past few days, but I couldn't bring myself to see her. I hoped that eventually I'd be able to pull myself together and tell her the whole story, but I just couldn't talk about it yet.

I was interrogated by the Mount Carmel Police, the New Haven Police and, of course, the Bridgeport Police. There wasn't much more I could tell them without implicating the Barnses and Leslie. So I didn't really give them that much. Instead I said that I had stumbled onto a few clues; that the murderer had decided to contact me and lead me from place to place by calling me on the phone.

There was one cop, though, who I told a little more to. That was Ivan (The Terrible) King. He didn't come on to me in his usual bullish way. Instead he respectfully told me how he had felt about Tommy. He claimed that he would make sure the Department took care of Tommy's family, and I shouldn't worry about it. It helped to know that. So I told Ivan a little more than I had the others. I was certain he'd never find the killer, but he looked so pathetic, trying to be so strong, assuring everyone on the force and in the media that it was only a matter of time before they apprehended the culprit. The way I saw it, at least he wasn't a fraud. He cared. Soon they would all forget Tommy, and Ivan could go back to what he did best—busting crack dealers and hookers.

Both the Bridgeport Post and the New Haven Register admitted, in a line or two, that there might have been a little improper journalism going on within the Fourth Estate. But the

THE FOURTH ESTATE MURDERS

effect it had on the overall episode was of no consequence. However, both papers had put up a reward for any information that might lead to the apprehension and conviction of the Fourth Estate Murderer.

Georgie hung black curtains over the windows of the Stayawhile and closed down. A number of the old-timers came up to my office, trying to get me to reason with Georgie and convince him to reopen because there was still more than a week to go before their pension checks came. Georgie always gave credit, and they'd pay monthly. Now there was nothing. They'd either have to stay home with their wives, or borrow money to go to another bar. It was all our fault—mine and Tommy's.

The first night after Tommy's death when I had done such a number on my office, wrecking just about everything, Leslie insisted that I sleep at her apartment. She had almost lost her job at the Post because of her involvement in the whole affair. It didn't matter because she'd quit anyway. She said that writing Tommy's obituary was out of the question. Instead she chose to go back to being a commercial artist where she could make things the way she wanted them. Leslie was warm, comforting, loving, and so much more.

The funeral was held at Our Lady of Good Council Church. Father Conklin, the priest who said the mass, was in semi-retirement—but he came out this day just for Tommy. He had been our C.Y.O. leader twenty-five years ago. Now he came to bury one of us, the one who had been crucified.

Everyone went over to Sally's house after the funeral. Kids were out in the back yard frolicking about. Inside, the house was jammed with people. I watched Sally talking with Leslie and Alice. My sisters were there. They were all getting to know each other a little better.

I drifted away. My brother-in-law, Frankie, grabbed me by the arm. "Come on, Jimmy, let's get you a drink."

Frankie had brought over all the food. "Hi, Frankie, thanks for all the food."

Crazy Lenny came over to join us. He pinched me on the cheek. "Hey, Jimmy? How da fuck are you? We been worried about ya."

"I'm okay, Len."

We walked over to the corner of the living room. Frankie asked, "What are you going to do, Jimmy?"

"I don't know."

Lenny grumbled, "I'll tell ya what he's gonna do. Find da bastard who took out Tommy and blow his fuckin' brains out."

Frankie seemed curious, "What's the guy like, Jimmy? The papers write about him as if he were supernatural."

I avoided the question, looking at Frankie. "There's nothing I can do. He's gone. I'm sure of it."

"Christ, Jimmy! He's going to get away with it?"

Lenny interrupted, "No fuckin' way. Jimmy's got a plan. He jus' don't want nobody to know what he's doin'. Right, Jimmy?"

I looked at Lenny. There were times when he could be brilliant, and at other times he was like a puppy dog. "No, Len. I have no plan. I haven't the slightest idea how to find the killer."

"How 'bout dat spade, Juju? I saw him at the cemetery. Didn't da cops pick him up for some of dese murders?"

I thought about it . . . no, it couldn't be Juju. Frankie grabbed my hand. "I kind of agree with Len. I never thought they should have let that Juju out of the can. Lenny told me that Louie Rosselli said Juju did it."

"No, Frankie, I'm almost positive Juju didn't do it. It isn't someone we know."

Lenny pointed over to the buffet table. "Look, ders Juju

freeloading a lunch."

I walked over to Juju. He was amassing a plate of food. As I approached I studied his face. He had so many white features; it occurred to me that it wouldn't be entirely impossible for him to impersonate a white person. He looked over at me. Seemingly startled, he put down his plate and threw his arms around me. "Jimmy, I'm so sorry about Tommy." I hugged him back, not saying anything. He asked, "Is there anything I can do?"

"No, but I'm glad you came."

"Well, I'll tell you, man, I almost didn't. Even though the papers say I was cleared of all charges, I didn't know how any of you would take my presence here." He looked very different from the last time I'd seen him. He always looked different from one time to the next. When he came to realize I was studying him he asked, "What's the matter, Jimmy? What are you doing?"

"Oh, I was just remembering that night when you were Abdul and I was James. It felt good pretending to be someone else, didn't it?"

"Hell, yes. All my life I've wanted to be someone else."

"What's wrong with being Juju?"

"Nothing, if you don't mind being half coon, half honky." All of a sudden Juju glanced at his watch. "Hey, I just remembered, I got to go." He reached for my hand, "Listen, Jimmy. You and Tommy are special to me. If there's anything I can do, don't hesitate to ask." He walked out. . . .

Later that day Leslie dropped me off at my office. I grabbed my mail and went inside. One of the letters had Barnes' Girdle and Bra logo on it. Inside there was a check for one thousand dollars and a short note: 'We are sorry about your tragic loss. Now your friend has joined our son. Neither one will be able to rest until this black-hearted, depraved creature is brought to justice'. . . I crumpled up the letter, threw it on the floor and scurried out of the office.

I found myself inside the Wagoneer, driving around Bridge-port. I was driving around the Beardsley Park area where Tommy and I grew up. There used to be a little fresh water beach and fewer than half as many houses. Now they were built almost one on top of the other. Instead of a beach there was the six-lane state highway on which I was driving. I saw Tommy's and my old houses standing next to one another. I pulled the Wagoneer over to the shoulder of the highway and got out. We used to be able to go down to the lake simply by crossing a bridle path. Now you have to cross the highway.

I walked down near the water which our two old houses faced. We had played here all the time, fishing for sunnies and perch, always making our families eat our catch—even though they hated the bony fish.

I remembered one day, at just about the end of the summer. Tommy and I had, for the whole season, ogled a girl named Bonnie. She was a few years older than we were. All the other boys used to mess around with her. Some said she was a whore. Back in those days, a whore could be a girl who allowed a boy to touch her.

Tommy and I had been fishing when he elbowed me and motioned with his head. I turned around and saw Bonnie opening up a blanket to lay down on. There was no one else around, just we three. We argued as to who was going to go and talk to her first. We both wanted to but were afraid. I got so nervous, I started to sweat. Tommy didn't notice because his knees were shaking. Finally I suggested, "Let's both talk to her together."

His face lit up. "You think she'll let us gang-bang her?"

I answered, "Maybe. You got your rubber with you?"

We both pulled out our wallets. Some time ago we had both

purchased Trojan contraceptives, just in case. Looking in the secret compartments of our wallets, we confirmed to each other that we were not only ready, but completely prepared for the adventure.

We started pushing each other to see who would go first. Then we almost got into a fight, which only started us giggling. So we walked up to Bonnie, taking some giant steps and some baby steps. She was laying on her stomach and didn't see us approaching. Her bathing suit had flowers on it. You could see the crack in her buttocks. We were standing over her quietly elbowing one another. Finally we spoke, "Hi."

She turned around, offering a superior gaze to our childish grins. But as she turned, one of her huge breasts also showed itself to our feasting eyes. Hoppy slid up my pants' leg, much more sure of its function than I was. "Hello, boys. I've seen you two around all summer. I'm Bonnie."

"Yes, we know. This is Jimmy, and I'm Tommy."

She handed us a bottle of Coppertone tanning lotion. "Would one of you mind putting some of this on my back?"

We both grabbed for the bottle, while she turned back onto her stomach. Tommy and I fought for the bottle, mouthing curses at one another. Finally after exchanging many dirty looks, he squirted some of the oil onto my hands and some onto his own. Before we knew it, we were both rubbing her back and legs. The best part was she didn't seem to mind at all.

Then Tommy asked one of the all-time greatest questions ever. "Do you want us to do your front, too, Bonnie?"

She turned completely around. Her bosom was gigantic. She must have been at least fifteen or sixteen years old. I was panting and drooling. She smiled, "Well, okay, but be careful where you touch. Don't get fresh."

I shook my head in complete surprise, "Who me, I'd never—I

mean . . . ah . . . um. Where can we touch?"

Tommy started to giggle. She looked up at me. "How old are you?"

I lied, "I'm almost fifteen. Why?"

"Aren't you two a little young to be interested in girls?"

I quickly began putting more oil in my hand before she changed her mind, and began applying it to her legs. Tommy answered, "No way! We like girls, especially you."

I was afraid to say anything, instead being content to spread the oil up and down one of her legs. Every time I'd go upwards I'd conquer more territory, getting closer to her furry area.

I felt crazy inside, but I couldn't have been as bad as Tommy because he blurted out a request I'll never forget. "Would you like me to put some oil on your tits?"

I turned away, choosing to look at her feet, afraid she was going to rudely dismiss us. But when I heard no rejection, I eventually got brave enough to turn back around. I couldn't believe my eyes, Tommy was kissing Bonnie and rubbing one of her big breasts. I grabbed his hand from one tit and placed it on the one that was closest to him. Then I put my face on the huge soft mound. Bonnie rubbed my head down on it. I hoped and thought that maybe she was one of those nymphomaniacs we had heard about. I was falling in love with her. Tommy was enjoying her other fun-bag while she brought me to her mouth. Her lips were wet and tasted better than anything I had ever had. She stuck her tongue in every possible part of my mouth. Hoppy, down below, ached so much that my ears were ringing. Then came the voice of authority from the other side of the bridle path. "Tommy! Tommy, come home!"

It was Tommy's mother calling for him. We both jumped up and ran for our fishing poles. By this time his mother was on our side of the bridle path and could now see Bonnie. We had our fishing poles and can of worms as we moved quickly to Mrs. Harrington—neither one of us even glancing in Bonnie's direction.

His mother asked, "What were you two up to? What have you been doing?"

I answered, "Nothing, Mrs. Harrington. Just fishing."

She looked down to where Bonnie had laid out her blanket, then gave me a slap on the rear-end, "You go home right now, Jimmy."

I ran to my house and hid behind a tree. I watched Tommy talking like crazy to his mother. I knew she'd tell my mother, but it had been worth it.

That night for the first time in my life, I had an orgasm. Hoppy had ached so much that I couldn't sleep. I kept on going to the bathroom to make sure it was alright. The head was almost purple and it had never gotten that big before. I didn't know what to do. I went back to bed, but I could only think of Bonnie and that tongue-kiss. Finally I lost control. Hoppy emitted burst after burst inside my underwear. I felt a little guilty, but it was inconsequential compared to the relief I experienced. The only problem was that I wanted to do it all over again. . . .

I left Beardsley Park thinking that Tommy would always be in my thoughts. I couldn't allow this thing to rest. The Barneses were paying me to find their son's killer, and that was just what I intended to try and do.

I returned to my office and began cleaning it up—putting everything away except for all the information I had on the killer and his victims. I looked at the note I had found under James Walblont's desk blotter. It was on the back of the flyer sent out by the Stratfield Theatre. I had never followed up on that. I had become so preoccupied with other phases of the investigation that it had just slipped my mind. It was time to pay the theater a visit.

The Stratfield Theatre was located in Stratford, Connecticut. It not only presented concerts and Shakespearean plays, but also had a Performing Arts Company.

When I pulled into the parking lot, there were quite a few cars on the grounds even though it was only the middle of the day. The theater looked like it had been a modern building in the 1950's era, but kind of funny looking in the 1990's. In any event, it had an attractiveness about it.

The front door was open so I walked right in. In the large lobby there were a few people working behind what looked to be a reception counter. Instead of going directly to them, I peeked inside the theater area. There was a whole cast rehearsing what was obviously a Shakespearean production. I looked long and hard at the people performing on stage, hoping I might be able to recognize one of them as "Harland, the biker". I thought, if necessary I'd question each one individually, but for now I'd go and see what I could learn from the people working behind the desk in the lobby.

There were two of them. One was a skinny, dark-haired, woman probably in her middle-to-late twenties. The other was, undoubtedly, a gay man who looked more feminine than the woman.

I leaned on the counter and spoke loudly, "Excuse me. My name is James Conte, I'm a private investigator looking for someone I'm told works here."

The gay man asked, "What can we do for you, Mr. Private Detective?"

I tried to hide my nervousness by speaking in a deep voice. "I'm not sure you can help me at all. Actually, I'm looking for several people. One is an ordinary-looking, black man with large feet. Another is a bearded man with a gold tooth who looks like

THE FOURTH ESTATE MURDERS

he's a member of the Hell's Angels. Two others I hardly have any description of other than one is a young Puerto Rican—medium height; the other is a slightly taller man wearing western clothes and probably from the southwest."

Neither seemed too interested in my questions—looking more interested in me. I hoped they wouldn't get too yucky and say things that would make me uncomfortable. I asked, "Do any of these I've mentioned ring a bell to you?"

The young lady responded, "Would you care for a cup of coffee?"

The gay man scolded her, "Oh, come now, Marly. He's here on business."

I figured I'd try a more authoritative approach. In a louder voice, I asked, "Do you have any Puerto Ricans in your company. Or any other Hispanics?"

They looked at each other saying at the same time, "No."

"How about southwestern cowboy types?"

This time they both shook their heads, no. "Any rough-looking men with beards, tatoos, or maybe gold teeth?"

He answered, "Oh, no, I'd remember that."

Marly giggled, while I continued, "How about black people, any in your company?"

They both nodded that there were, with Marly saying, "We need more information before we answer any more questions."

I looked at them, trying to be as sincere as possible. "They are all entitled to an insurance claim, that's all. I have money to give to these people. Won't you help?"

Marly answered, "I'll help. We have two black men in our company."

The gay man added, "Yes, but as far as I know neither one has extraordinarily large feet."

I asked, "Is either one in the theater now?"

He answered, "No, they are not in the cast of Hamlet. They are both trying out for the lead in Othello. Whoever loses becomes the understudy."

"Oh. Do you have their names and telephone numbers by any chance?"

Marly explained, "I don't know if we should give you that information without first conferring with them."

I pulled a hundred dollar bill out of my pocket and put it on the counter. The gay man looked impressed, "Aren't we Mr. Money Bags. Is this how you get everything you want, by paying for it?"

I pulled out another hundred. "Can I please have their names and numbers?"

She grabbed both bills, while he got the directory. I pulled out my pad and pen, ready to write down the information. He offered, "One is named Nat Wright and he lives in the theater house, only a block away from here. I live there, also."

I jotted down the name and number while he looked up the listing for the other black man. "The other is a local fellow named Abdul Salam. He lives in Bridgeport."

He was giving me the phone number, but I was paying no attention. For what? I would have bet just about anything that Abdul was Juju. I remembered the last thing he had said to me—'If there is anything I can do to help, don't hesitate to ask.'

I stared blankly at them; they were both looking back at me, waiting. The man smiled, "Earth to Mr. Conte; Earth calling Mr. Conte."

I snapped out of it, asking, "When does this Othello production take place?"

Marly answered, "Not until the end of spring. That's quite some time from now."

"What do they do in the meantime?"

THE FOURTH ESTATE MURDERS

The man answered, "In the winter, most members of our company go to Key West, Florida for roles in productions there. I know that Nat Wright is down there, or on his way down. But I'm not sure about Abdul. I saw him less than a week ago—but that doesn't mean anything. I can tell you this, the Key West Playhouse is putting on a production of Othello and you could probably make a good bet that Abdul will try out for it."

I had to be sure. I gave Marly and the man a complete description of Abdul. They both agreed; I had identified Abdul better than they could have. . . .

For a week I searched the streets of Bridgeport, looking for Juju. He was nowhere to be found. I still didn't believe Juju was the killer. It just didn't fit, unless he had an accomplice. I would keep on telling myself that there was no way that Juju could have killed Tommy. I might have been wrong about a lot of things, like believing that at almost forty years old I still had a chance to make it in the Major Leagues—but I didn't think I was wrong about Juju. I couldn't be. . . .

I had pretty much moved in with Leslie. Love was in bloom again. She was wonderful. Even my ex-wife, Sally, and my daughters liked her. Everything would have been as good as it gets if Tommy had still been alive. But he wasn't. If I was going to put my life in order, I had to find Tommy's murderer and bring him to justice.

FIFTEEN

Gina Cataliano had been in the lower Florida Keys for almost two weeks now. She had come down to the Keys for rest and relaxation. She had no intention of looking for an affair with a man, even though she was an attractive southern-Italian woman from an outlying area near the Tyrrehenian Sea. People asked her to delight them with her wonderful Italian accent. Her rich black hair was cut short but remained her most striking feature. All her clothes looked as if they were imported from Italy. She wore them as if they had been designed just for her. No man in the southern Keys could claim that he had been intimate with Gina, even though a few contended they had anyway. That didn't mean that Gina couldn't sit at one of those funky, Key, conch bars with several men and have a great time. Sometimes she'd even do some heavy kissing with one, as long as he kept his hands off her. She liked kissing, she knew her men friends liked it, but she never stayed around long enough for one of the men to violate her body.

Even though she frequented much of the Lower Keys, it was Key West that she really enjoyed. One of the men she had kissed and drunk with at a bar told her that Key West people called themselves Conchs. He claimed though, they had nothing but nuts and bolts inside their heads. And he had been right, but she loved it, simply loved Key West.

Gina had gotten into the habit of spending the mornings and early afternoons alone, reading and sunbathing. She claimed, to any would-be suitors, that the reading helped her practice her English and was also very relaxing. She, more than anyone, knew how much she needed the rest.

She had also gotten into the habit of biking everyday in the late afternoon into Olde Key West. She'd usually stop at the Half Shell Raw Bar, get something to eat, and flirt with the two bartenders on duty. Then she would bike over to Duval Street and do a little window shopping until the early singing groups started at Sloppy Joe's. Usually there would be an early afternoon group singing folk songs of the Sixties and Seventies. Then from five to nine there would be a country rock group. And at nine to closing, Sloppy Joe's would feature hard rock. . . .

I had just about convinced myself that Juju had indeed gone to Key West to try out for his Shakespearean role. I flirted with the idea of going down after him—if for no other reason than perhaps to get some answers to my questions. Besides, I was getting nowhere up here. I figured I'd give the Stratfield Theatre one more try. Maybe Juju had shown up there, or someone else that might be related to the case.

Only the gay man was at the counter on this day. I reintroduced myself and refreshed his memory about the types of people I was looking for. He claimed nobody like them had been around the theater since he'd been working there. He also claimed he hadn't seen Juju since my last visit.

I asked, "Do you have any kind of list of the members in your company who have gone down to work at the Key West Playhouse?"

"Well, yes, we do, but I'm not sure I should show it to you."

I reached into my pocket for money but he waved me off saying, "Please, Mr. Conte, I'm not a leech. I'll read off the names to you, okay?"

ED CALANDRO

I nodded while he began. The list must have been in alphabetical order because after three or four names he said, "Bruno Cataliano."

I stopped him, "Wait! Did you say Bruno Cataliano?"

He nodded, "Why, yes. But Bruno is no actor, he does make-up."

"Do you recall what he looks like?"

"Of course. Very dark complected, blotchy whiskers, thick curly hair and a dynamite body."

I remembered the name Bruno Cataliano easily. His wife, Gina had come to my office just before this whole thing had started. I had forgotten all about her. The attractive Italian woman who had offered an inviting alternative to vaginal sex. Her husband Bruno was beating her for no particular reason. She had wanted me to find out where he went on Saturdays. Now, nearly a month later, I would find out just that.

I decided I'd go home and pack a bag. I was going to the Keys as soon as possible. . . .

I told Leslie all about my plans. She insisted on coming along with me but, as persistant as she was, I knew she had no chance of convincing me. I tried to reason with her, "Look, Les, I've got to do this on my own. You have to trust me . . . that I'm capable."

She gave me a forlorn look, "Well, I don't. Anybody who believes he has a chance of being a Major League baseball player at the age of thirty-nine shouldn't be going up against such a monstrous person alone."

"I'm sorry you ever learned about the baseball thing. I'll bet you'll never let me forget it."

She pleaded, "No, don't you see, that's what I like about you, you're harmless. I remember when Tommy told me you couldn't even shoot the targets at the police academy."

I had my bag just about packed. I said, "Look, I need you up here, Leslie." I threw some money on the table. "Will you see that Sally gets this just in case I'm not back right away."

She folded her arms, looking quite upset with me. "What about this Gina thing?"

"What do you mean?"

"You know what I mean. What if she sticks her naked derrière in front of you again? Are you going to tell me that you will turn it down?

It felt good to think that maybe she was a little bit jealous, but it was important that she knew exactly how I felt. "I'm going down there to look for Tommy's murderer. That's it. But Leslie, I'll do whatever it takes to find the son-of-a-bitch."

Her voice softened, "That's what I'm afraid of."

"How about you up here?"

"What do you mean?"

"You know, another guy."

"God, Jimmy. Until you came along I hadn't been with another man for a year and a half. What do you think I'm going to do, grab the milkman as soon as you walk out the door?"

It had been a long time since I'd won an argument with anybody. I couldn't quite figure if I had actually won this one or if Leslie had just let me think I had. However, she conceded. I told her where my insurance policy was in the office. I even had the courage to ask her if she'd visit Sally and the girls every now and then. She assured me she would. There was only one more thing Leslie had to do before she would allow me to go. She opened up her couch and gave me a session in love-making unequaled in all my days. I wasn't sure if it was meant to satisfy me or her until I got back. Maybe it was some of both. . . .

This was Juju's first visit to the Florida Keys. He had been a member of a number of theater companies, but he had never traveled this far for a part. Now he was on the verge of getting the starring role in Othello. His only competition was the respected black actor, Nat Wright. If Nat Wright hadn't made the trip, then Juju wouldn't have either. But that wasn't the case. He figured that whoever got the part here at the Key West Playhouse would also star this spring at the Stratfield Theatre.

Being a native of Bridgeport, and an exceptional athlete besides, didn't allow him much opportunity to share his dramatic goals with most of his friends and family. He usually traveled to all-white communities like Westport or Silvermine, Connecticut to fulfill his acting needs.

Although he had never met his white father, he had heard from his Aunt Marjorie that his father was also in show business. But that's all he knew about him. He supposed it was from his father that he had acquired this innate desire to act. After years of lying about where he came from and many times pretending to be someone else, like Abdul Salam, he was close to landing his first major role as Othello, the Moor of Venice. . . .

Gina Cataliano didn't care that much for hard rock music. But she did enjoy the groups featured earlier at Sloppy Joe's. There was the usual daytime folk singers who were always a delight after a day of sun and fun. But during this particular week, it was necessary to get to Sloppy Joe's early because performing from five to nine was one of Key West's favorites, Wild Bill Daily. The club would start filling up about four o'clock.

Gina liked to get there around three-thirty so she could get a seat at the bar, facing the stage. All the employees at Sloppy Joe's knew her. She was attractive, liked music, and certainly liked to drink. But what made her stand out even more was the

THE FOURTH ESTATE MURDERS

fact that she liked to drink her beers through a straw.

Sloppy Joe's usually had two bouncers during the day and three at night. Naturally, Gina knew them all. They were there to keep trouble from starting. However, this one evening just before Wild Bill Daily was about to start his second set, the three bouncers came rushing toward her. The biggest of the bouncers was named Jaws. He had a shaven, tanned head, gleaming white teeth when he showed his nasty smile, and tatoos all over his hairy arms and fingers.

Jaws pointed down at the top of the head of a young man sitting near Gina. A bartender nodded 'yes' and the three bouncers, led by Jaws, yanked the young man up off his bar stool, carried him to the doors and threw him out. On the way back to his position, Jaws gave the stunned Gina a big, white-toothed, macho smile. Gina was in a state of despair. Wild Bill had started singing, with the people screaming and singing along with him and his band. But not Gina, she wondered what the young man could have done to be thrown out so rudely.

She got off of her bar stool and glanced at Jaws, who continued smiling at her as she was leaving. Walking to her bicycle she could still hear Wild Bill Daily and his fans, singing, "One, two three, what are we fighting for? Don't ask me I don't give a damn; next stop is Viet Nam."

The next day Gina decided to go back to Sloppy Joe's and catch Wild Bill Daily's final show at the club. She had just ordered her first beer. The bartenders enjoyed unwrapping her straw and putting it into her beer before they served her.

Sloppy Joe's was still filling up with people. She knew it would be jam-packed for Wild Bill's farewell performance.

The bouncers either walked through the crowd or stood perched on platforms a few feet higher than the floor. This way they could get a better view of the goings-on and see when anyone of them might need help from the others. Jaws had found it difficult to concentrate on his job; instead lustfully admiring the attractive Italian woman sitting at the bar.

Gina had become well aware of the lascivious glances of Jaws. But it was a busy night at the club and both were distracted by other activities. Suddenly it became necessary for Jaws to bully his way through the crowd to a troublesome customer, grabbing the drunken man around the neck while another bouncer pulled on the drunk's arm. In almost no time they had him out of the door and back on Duval Street.

These barbaric tactics upset Gina no end. It was like legalized violence. She was beginning to get herself all worked up when she was pleasantly interrupted by a dizzy-looking, blond-haired, young man. He spoke like a California beach-dude, "Hey, chick."

She offered him a friendly smile, "Buona sera."

He seemed confused, "Huh?"

She thought he looked like he had been out in the sun for too long.

He smiled, showing off his white teeth and handsome face. "Hi, I'm TT." He pointed to the straw sticking out of her beer. "Way-cool, babe!"

She would need to speak her best English, "Mi no understand, waya-cool."

He laughed, not believing her, "Come on, you know, AWE-SOME!! FAR-OUT!! What's your name, babe?"

She laughed, "Mi name Gina. Please calla mi Gina."

"For sure." He then yelled to the bartender, "Hey dude! Two brews here."

She liked this young man, TT. It wasn't difficult to figure out that he was a surfer-type. That's how they all talked and looked.

As soon as the beers were served, TT reached over and grabbed a straw for himself. This maneuver further delighted

THE FOURTH ESTATE MURDERS

Gina.

Now, for a while, they were unable to speak because Wild Bill Daily had begun his first set of music. And when Wild Bill and his band played, there were only three things you could do, sing along, listen, or dance. Gina and TT did some of all three. It was fun—good, simple pleasure. However, from time to time she could not help glancing Jaws' way. She could see that he was watching her while she danced. She wondered if TT would be Jaws' next victim of brutality.

In Sloppy Joe's as long as you kept your drink on the bar in front of your bar stool, that seat was yours for as long as you wanted it. So when Wild Bill and his good ole boys finished their first set, TT and Gina returned to their bar stools. TT looked a little extra dizzy. She asked, "What-sa di matter? You hav sick?"

"No, wahini. All this dancing. It's like being gassed out by a wave."

It had only been a few moments since Wild Bill had put down his guitar when he walked back on stage and tapped on the microphone, testing to see if it was on. His deep, rich, southern voice roared over the P.A. system, "Hey, you, mamas and papas, we'all just got the dawg-gon' word: the mother of all dang wars is over! Our boys'ill be comin' home soon!"

Everybody in Sloppy Joe's screamed with joy. Gina got so excited she planted a delicious kiss on the lips of TT. Wild Bill waved for the exuberant audience to calm down, finally saying, "The word out of the Middle East is, Saddam claims et weren't all the bombin' that made him surrender. Hell, he was in a bunker, five stories below ground level! Saddam said et was the goddam blockade that ended et." Wild Bill wiped the sweat off his face, speaking even louder, "He ran out of fuckin' toilet paper! As much as that son-of-a-bitch been shitin' these days, no wonder he called et quits!" He yelled even louder, "Everybody swill-up! Sloppy Joe's is gonna buy ya'll a drink." That brought on applause more deafening than those for the end of the war.

TT asked, "Hey, Gina, Why's that big, ugly dude scrunting us?"

Gina looked over at Jaws, who was perched a few feet higher than everyone else. "Oh, TT, he mi friend. No worry."

TT excused himself and went off to the men's room.

Jaws noticed Gina looking his way. He gave her a big, toothy smile. She returned it with a sexy look. They hardly took their eyes off one another as she made her way through the packed house to where he had stationed himself. With two beers in her hand, she walked right up to him, pretending to be a little drunker than she was. Jaws grabbed one of the beers and roared, "Thank ya, honey. I was wonderin' when ya'd be comin' my way."

She tried to act a little helpless and as sexy as she could, "Mi no think-a you see mi."

He grabbed her around the waist, easily lifting her up high, saying, "Git rid o' that faggot ya been playin' with, or I'll git rid o' him fer ya."

She showed him an angry face. "Jaws! You let-a mi down, now."

"What's the matter, honey? Ya don't like et?" He let her down.

She was quick to make him forget her anger. She pulled the straw out of her beer and put the head of the bottle to her mouth, fondling it with her lips as if it were a male organ. She said, "Mi like you touch-a mi. But no here. All di people they think-a maybe mi di whore." She never took the bottle away from her mouth.

Jaws knew he had his bouncer work to do, but he couldn't help himself. He asked, "Are ya gonna wait fer me tonight?"

She cooed, "Mi no think-a mi can."

He felt a little puzzled and angry, wondering if she was thinking about returning to the surfer dope. "C'mon, honey, ya kin wait fer me."

She placed her hand on Jaws' hairy, tattooed arm, "Mi no think-a mi can wait that-a long for you."

Jaws titled his head to one side like a confused dog. Gina suggested, "Why you no ask-a you friends to watch-a di Sloppy Joe's for you? We go out for a little bit."

His toothy smile gleamed, "Good idea. I'll tell 'em we'll be back in about twenty minutes."

Gina abruptly ordered, "No! You tell-a them maybe one hour, maybe more."

As soon as they got outside, Gina explained to Jaws that she was having her period. The "flower" between her legs was all messy and he should not touch it. She also clarified that her tettas were very sore from her delicate condition and he shouldn't touch them either. Jaws looked confused and asked, "Well then, what in hell kin I touch?"

They had just turned the corner at an abandoned, brick building right next to Sloppy Joe's. As soon as they were out of view of the street, Gina placed her hand between Jaws' legs, and said, "You no hav-a to touch nothing. Mi do all-a di touch."

Earlier that day, Gina had already figured out how to get inside the abandoned building, but she still asked, "You know-a how to get inside this place?"

He grumbled, "Ya bet yer sweet ass I do."

They sneaked in through the back entrance. As soon as they got inside, Jaws wanted to start right in on her. But Gina tugged on Jaws' hand, leading him all the way to the top of the building, three flights up. When they finally reached the top they could barely hear Wild Bill and his band, who had started their next set.

ED CALANDRO

All the boarded-up windows made it dark, but a few rays of the setting sun slipped through the cracks of the slowly eroding building. Jaws could wait no longer. He pulled Gina to himself and planted a whale of a kiss on her. She tried to pull away, but it was useless. She just hoped he wouldn't feel the .45 she had strapped just above her knee.

When he let her go, she began to rub his penis feverishly, hoping this would momentarily satisfy him and he wouldn't try to grab her in a bear-hug again. As soon as she had gotten it worked up, almost hard, he was hers. He stood still, like a pet gorilla, until she had his organ stroked to maximum size.

Gina, proud of the simplicity it took to control this man, spoke in a sexually-aroused tone of voice, "It's so big-a and hard. Mi don't know where to put it." She unzipped him and pulled it out of his pants.

Jaws moaned, "Why don't ya just go 'head and suck on et?" *'Ssure fatssso, good idea.'*

Gina reached up her dress and pulled out the .45 with one hand, while squeezing Jaws' balls as hard as she could with the other hand. As soon as Jaws' mouth opened to scream, Gina stuck the .45 inside it and yelled, "Why don't you suck-a some-a this hot lead." BANG.

Parts of Jaws' head were blown away, but the convenient placement of the .45 inside his mouth helped to muffle the sound of the gunshot. Besides that, they were on the third floor of an abandoned building.

She stripped the corpse of all of its valuable belongings, which wasn't much. But Jaws had numerous identification cards, and they were invaluable. As far as her performance went, she thought she hadn't done such a bad job considering she'd had to "ad-lib" most of the way.

She moved quickly to exit the building, thinking it was time to teach a few more bouncers a good lesson. But as much as she liked the roles of Gina and her husband, Bruno, she would have to forsake any further use of either character for quite some time.

The abandoned building had its own parking lot, but it was usually full with the cars of Sloppy Joe's patrons. Her bicycle was chained to a pole between the two buildings, so she wouldn't have to go back out front and be seen by anyone who might have observed her leaving with Jaws. As much as she would have liked to have seen the final set of Wild Bill and the boys, that was now out of the question. In another thirty or so minutes, Jaws would be considered missing. It could possibly be days before they found his body, but she couldn't take that chance. She would have to check out of where she was staying and take up a new residence and a new persona.

Gina moved quickly across the parking lot to her bike. She noticed the obscure figure of a fair-haired man coming her way. Twilight had become dusk. She realized who it was—that sun-baked dope, TT. There was, at the moment, no one else in the parking lot. She knew she didn't have much time, she would have to eliminate him also.

TT looked so happy to have found her. "Hey, wahini. Where have you been."

"Oh, TT, mi hav big problema, please come?"

TT followed Gina as she changed directions and turned back toward the abandoned building. He asked, "What's the matter, babe?"

She made sure he could hear, although she whispered, "Mi fica, mi fica all wet." She continued leading the way, with her back to him.

TT, confused, asked, "What in the heck is *mi fica*?"

She turned, offering a sensual look, "It mi pussy, mi pussy all wet."

TT's eyes crossed as he became ga-ga, "Gnarly! Out of control, wahini."

She pointed to the same place she and Jaws had used to enter the building. But she momentarily slowed down while another man walked across the street, coming from the opposite direction. She would have to wait until he passed before she could lead TT into the building. . . .

Juju prepared himself for the impact. This would be for Bridgeport and all those who remembered how it used to be. This was for those days when everybody thought for sure that he would be a professional football player, even though theatrics was his love. . . .

Gina fumbled for her .45 as the man moved closer. She'd have to shoot him, it was all becoming too dangerous. . . .

TT grabbed Gina from behind. For a moment she thought it was a misguided gesture of lust. But then he tightened his grip on her. At almost the same moment the other man stepped up and drove his fist hard into the face of Gina. He hit her again and again. . . .

TT threw her up against the wall, pinning her there. He had been the recipient of a punch or two from Juju himself at one time or another, so he knew how Gina felt. He pulled off his blond wig, while Juju held onto the murderer. She was almost insensible from Juju's punches, but still aware enough to hear the man who had been disguised as TT say, "Gnarly, huh? One way-cool acting job. Right, dog-shit." Having thus identified himself, Jimmy drove his fist hard between the false bosom of the disguised madman, who wilted into Juju's grasp, then slid to the ground.

Juju realized he had better take control of the situation. "Come on, Jimmy we'd better get this thing out of here before the fuzz take notice."

They hoisted up the limp body and braced it between themselves. Then they walked to Jimmy's Wagoneer, making-believe that the figure between them was drunk, out cold—and that they, were heavily intoxicated themselves.

SIXTEEN

I opened the back door of the Wagoneer, while Juju threw the almost-unconscious form into it. We had prepared ourselves for this, with ropes and a gag for the mouth. After we tied up this enigma, I started up the Wagoneer's engine. Juju was standing outside my window. "Hey, man. Why don't you just turn him over to the Florida police and be done with it?"

"I can't, Juju. I have to take him back to Bridgeport. Some lawyer down here might be able to find a way to keep him in Florida . . . who knows . . . but I believe they'll hang his ass in Bridgeport.

Juju sighed, "Yeah, maybe you're right, Jimmy. You'd better get the hell out of here before somebody sees us."

"What are you going to do?"

"I'm staying here, man. I told you, I'm going to get that part of Othello."

Juju's hand was on my door. I placed mine on top of his, saying, "This was for Tommy."

He smiled, "Yeah, man, for Tommy. Now get the hell out of here and don't break the speed limits." He turned and left. My passenger and I did the same.

Driving out of the Keys and southern Florida was difficult because of all the traffic. But once I hit central Florida, I cruised at seventy-five miles per hour with plenty of cars passing me, so I wasn't worried about being nailed for speeding.

Every once in a while I'd feel my passenger move a little. He was laid out on the floor of the back seat. There wasn't much he could do, being securely bound and gagged. Whenever I stopped for gas, I just threw a blanket over him so no one would notice him.

I thought about the past few days. It hadn't taken me long to find Juju. He was working at the Key West Playhouse. I learned that Bruno Cataliano came to the playhouse every morning for no apparent reason, since the playhouse was not showing any kind of production at the moment. We guessed he was just staying in touch with playhouse activities.

The next morning, Juju and I followed Bruno to a small trailer on Boca Chica Key, the next island up from Key West. Juju then returned to the playhouse, while I stayed on stake-out. Soon Gina came out and biked all the way into Key West, making her rounds, and finally ending up at Sloppy Joe's. She did this for two days in a row before Juju decided to make me up to look like a surfer-type. His coaching was phenomenal. He taught me to become the surfer; for if I didn't, it might cost me my life. I embraced the role. The only one I was worried I wouldn't be able to fool was Gina. But I was convinced that I had done so when I followed her and Jaws to the abandoned building. I didn't see it, but I knew she had killed Jaws. After I had heard the gun shot, I retreated to the rear parking lot and it was there that Juju and I set our own little trap. . . .

I was hoping I'd be able to drive non-stop to Bridgeport. Every time I stopped for gas, I bought a cup of coffee. It helped to keep me awake, but also gave me the shakes. Lately my passenger had been emitting a little gas. I was worried he might discharge some excrement on the floor of my car. The odor began to really bother me, so I decided to risk it and take him outside to relieve himself. I waited until we were in a remote area of Georgia, then drove off the Interstate into a swampy, wooded area. I grabbed my flashlight and pulled my captive out of the Wagoneer, his black wig had fallen off revealing a white head with no more than peach fuzz for hair.

The moon was almost full as I pulled him behind some bushes. I kept his hands tied behind his back and his mouth still gagged. I untied his feet and legs so I could pull down his tight, female jeans for him. I said, "Alright, you only have five minutes, so if you want to shit, you better do it quick."

After I had slowly removed the jeans. I shined my flashlight down at him while he squatted. I couldn't believe my eyes. He had nothing between his legs, no vagina, no penis—only a pee-hole. I looked down at him; he coldly stared back. A chill ran through my body. I thought to myself that God had dealt this what-ever-it-was, a cruel hand.

I moved just in time to avoid his foot which was aimed at my face. It wasn't too difficult to subdue him, as he was still bound. First I pinned his neck up against a tree, then forced him to squat down while I did the same still holding him. Then I ordered, "Alright, take your shit now." And he did, with me holding my hand against his neck while we stared at one another under the moon-lit Georgia night. . . .

By the time we entered the Carolinas, the sun had been up for quite some time. I pulled into a fast-food restaurant that had a drive-in window. I got us both some food, then just before we got back on the Interstate I turned the captive over so he'd be face down. This way he could eat without being untied and I wouldn't have to hand-feed him.

I listened while it munched the food off the floor. The fact that it wasn't gagged, frightened me. I didn't know what I'd do if this personality parade started talking about Tommy. Then I blurted it out. A question that had troubled me all through the night. "What are you, a man or a woman?"

I could hear that it had stopped eating, but there was no response. There was such an eerie sensation within the Wagoneer. Then a deep-toned, masculine voice said, "Which do you prefer me to be, a male or a female? I can be whatever you like or whatever you want." I said nothing, waiting for it to continue. "Hey, shit-for-brains, what is it ye want, for me to fuck ye up the ass . . . or . . .'scusi mi, you hav-a mi bend over like-a in you office and sodomita mi."

I suddenly realized that even before Remsen Barnes had hired me, this one on the Wagoneer's floor had already prepared itself for the challenge. Bugging the Barneses home had made it easy to ascertain their every move. No doubt when they had decided to hire me, the character of Gina had preceded Mr. Barnes to my office to plant a bug there also. The fact that the Gina character chose to be there when Mr. Barnes arrived only made me realize just how confident this fiend was with its omnipotence in the portrayal of its characters.

I had heard of asexual people, but I had thought their organs were removed by surgery, rather than being born without any. The very idea of not having a sex organ was unfathomable. Then from behind my seat came the voice, "Hey, Jimmy, when are you going to untie these freakin' ropes?"

My foot slammed on the brakes as I veered off to the shoulder of the Interstate. "TOMMY! No, it can't be!"

I stopped the Wagoneer and looked behind my seat only to see my captive laying face down. I yanked at the impostor, flipping him over, seeing a satisfied smile on his face. I shook so much I could hardly speak, but finally whispered hoarsely, "What has made you so cruel?

The next voice was indistinguishable, "I do not know, for I

seek out cruelty and destroy it before it escalates." He was babbling.

It sounded like both a male and female. I thought about this thing behind me. If it could somehow untie itself, I would surely be dead. I retied the gag around its mouth, then checked to make sure the knots in the bonds were secure. I had to get this thing to the Bridgeport police.

I thought about the news media. They would hype this story nation-wide. Who knew how many people this thing had killed—and for what reasons? Soon his actions would be center stage and I couldn't help but think that's what it had wanted all along.

SEVENTEEN

I arrived in Bridgeport about three in the morning. The streets were wet with a late-winter rainfall. I believed my captive was asleep. The only people out on the streets were some motley hookers and a few of the homeless. I was only a block away from the police station but decided to wait until later that morning to turn in my prisoner. This way I could possibly slip him to Ivan King and maybe avoid prosecution for the various crimes that I had probably committed.

I had not slept in over twenty-four hours, but I wasn't tired anymore. I drove around the city, going no place in particular. I found myself driving along the coast near Long Island Sound. It was there that I realized Tommy and I had earned our promised reward. I stopped at a telephone booth and called the Barneses, telling them that I had captured their son's murderer and was waiting until later in the morning to turn him in. Mrs. Barnes suggested I should come to their house and wait. I thought that was a good idea, and headed for St. Mary's by the Sea.

The outside lights at the Barneses home were the only ones on. I pulled into their driveway. A moment later Mr. Barnes came out to greet me. Even at this early hour he had a regal air about him. He took my hand, saying, "Well done, son. We have been worried about you, but always remaining confident you would prevail." He looked inside the Wagoneer, asking, "Where is he?"

"Well, Mr. Barnes, it is not exactly a he, but it's in the back seat of my car."

He didn't even question my statement, simply ordering, "Come, let us bring him inside."

"Do you think that would be a good idea, Mr. Barnes? It might be too upsetting for Mrs. Barnes. Besides, this thing is very dangerous."

"Mrs. Barnes needs to see him before you turn him over to the police."

I was way too tired to argue. So I carefully opened the back door and pulled the killer out, practically dragging him along as Mr. Barnes led the way inside his house. I didn't think this was a very good idea, but there wasn't much I could or wanted to do about it.

We walked into the same living room where I had been seated during my other visits with the Barneses. Mrs. Barnes was there waiting. Her eyes were already fixed on my captive. Without turning she said to me, "I am pleased you were not harmed, Mr. Conte." But when my captive, whom I thought was devoid of strength saw Mrs. Barnes, it struggled with all it's power to pull away from me.

She moved closer to it, still staring, "Yes, you have caught this thing. This killer of all that is good. Untie him, he looks so uncomfortable."

I wanted to inform her that it possibly wasn't a he, but I was becoming just as frightened of her as I was of my captive. Mr. Barnes began undoing the knots to release the ropes of my captive. Mrs. Barnes was in front of us now, ordering, "Take a firm hold, Mr. Conte. We wouldn't want this slippery, slimy thing to slither free."

I put a strong grip on my prisoner; as I did, I felt the tension leave its body. It offered no resistance, instead looking Mrs. Barnes directly in the eyes, reciting, "If I could pray to move, prayers would move me: But I am constant as the Northern Star."

THE FOURTH ESTATE MURDERS

I was getting panicky. The voice was like no other I had heard it use. It was a man's voice, deep and rich, possibly with a touch of an English accent. He sounded like he was doing Shakespeare.

Mr. Barnes joined his wife in front of the killer. Now he, too, was staring. Mrs. Barnes said, "Oh, you certainly will become a celebrity. You sound so interesting. I'm sure you'll be able to tell over and over again the stories of your contemptible deeds. I know you will become famous, and that's what you want, isn't it?"

Looking from her wrath to his, it spoke, "The skies are painted with unnumbered sparks, they are all fire and everyone doth shine." It was acting! It was doing Shakespeare.

She nodded her head in agreement, "Yes, you are right." She pulled from inside her nightdress a large kitchen knife. Waving it, she continued, "Here is some more truth. This useless, burning flame standing before me shall be snuffed out forevermore. Take this for my Morgan and all those others you have unmercifully killed."

She ran him through with the sharp weapon. He jolted and quivered in my arms. She held her hand on the knife whose blade lay deep within our prisoner. She turned to her husband, tears rolling down her cheeks. "Let this thing feel your contempt, Remsen."

The normally regal-looking man also had tears in his eyes. He placed his hand on his wife's and together they twisted the blade violently, churning the captive's insides.

This thing, who had murdered many good people, was now fading fast. I hardly needed to hold him, the Barneses held him up with the knife. Mrs. Barnes looked over at me, probably noticing the fear and uncertainty on my face. She reached with her free hand, and grabbing one of mine, intoned, "Come, Jim Conte, let this one feel your hurt."

ED CALANDRO

She placed my hand on the handle of the knife along with her husband's and her's. The murderer gazed at me, it's eyes had become as docile as a lamb's. It wanted to continue its performance right to the end. It began, "Et tu. . . ." But the three of us twisted and turned the blade so savagely that we took its words, and life away—forever.

It was crazy, but I thought of Tommy looking down at me remembering when I couldn't even shoot at a target. "Rest in peace, my brother. . . ."

Mr. Barnes and I took the body to the east side of Bridgeport. It would soon be daylight, so we had to hurry. When we were discussing what we should do with the killer's body, Mrs. Barnes had suggested, nonchalantly, "Throw it in a dumpster, nobody will miss it." So that's what we did. The dumpster in the parking lot of Jenny's Famous Hot Dogs.

I called Ivan King and informed him as to where the body was. I'm sure he knew it was me doing the talking because I didn't disguise my voice, but he never acknowledged it during our conversation. The next day I read where he said he had received an anonymous tip. I thought, Tommy had been right, he was a good man.

The Barneses had been true to their promise. They paid me, one hundred thousand dollars. I immediately paid off the mortgage on Tommy's house and part of Sally's. Tommy's wife, Alice was so pleased to finally see me, she hugged and kissed me like I was a long lost brother. At last we were able to weep for Tommy in one another's arms.

There was still some money left over, most of which I gave to Alice and Sally. They were single mothers, raising children. Knowing these two ladies, and after the incident with Mrs. Barnes, I came to believe that the whole world was moved by mothers.

I saved a little of the money for Leslie and me, not that either one of us was in any great need of money. We had each other, and it seemed like that was much more than either of us had expected at this stage of our lives. What I saved the money for was a little vacation for us down in Key West, Florida. Juju was starring as Othello, the Moor of Venice. He was given the role when his main competition, Nat Wright, had mysteriously disappeared.

I had to admit that a few things had definitely changed in my way of thinking. All of a sudden Bridgeport didn't look so bad. My family and friends lived here. I kind of got the feeling that those who had stayed in Bridgeport were a little stronger than most other folks. It wasn't such a bad place if you looked at the brighter side of things—like, there wouldn't be so much smog nowadays since so many of the factories had closed down.

Then there was the other thing—the realization that I wasn't going to be a Major League ball player. Jeez, most other people would have figured that out in their teens. But then again, I hadn't realized I was a pretty good detective, either. That's all there was to it. Everybody needed something to be good at.